D0782950

SPECIAL MESSAGE TO READERS

THE ULVERSCROFT FOUNDATION
(registered UK charity number 264873)
was established in 1972 to provide funds for research, diagnosis and treatment of eye diseases. Examples of major projects funded by the Ulverscroft Foundation are:-

- The Children's Eye Unit at Moorfields Eye Hospital, London
- The Ulverscroft Children's Eye Unit at Great Ormond Street Hospital for Sick Children
- Funding research into eye diseases and treatment at the Department of Ophthalmology, University of Leicester
- The Ulverscroft Vision Research Group, Institute of Child Health
- Twin operating theatres at the Western Ophthalmic Hospital, London
- The Chair of Ophthalmology at the Royal Australian College of Ophthalmologists

You can help further the work of the Foundation by making a donation or leaving a legacy. Every contribution is gratefully received. If you would like to help support the Foundation or require further information, please contact:

THE ULVERSCROFT FOUNDATION
The Green, Bradgate Road, Anstey
Leicester LE7 7FU, England
Tel: (0116) 236 4325

website: www.foundation.ulverscroft.com

MYSTERY IN MOON LANE

What could be the explanation for that strange affair of the corpse in old-fashioned clothing, taken from a burning building in Moon Lane by rescuers during the Blitz, Christmas 1940? Who is the mysterious young woman who models for young artist Jevons as he paints in a haze? What is the myth of the seal woman, and should Dan and his wife Leonora be afraid? Ghosts, myths and ancient curses are the subjects of six stories from the pen of A.A. Glynn.

Books by A. A. Glynn
in the Linford Mystery Library:

CASE OF THE DIXIE GHOSTS

A. A. GLYNN

MYSTERY IN MOON LANE

Complete and Unabridged

LINFORD
Leicester

First published in Great Britain

First Linford Edition
published 2014

Copyright © 2002, 2003, 2004, 2008, 2013
by Anthony A. Glynn
All rights reserved

*A catalogue record for this book is available
from the British Library.*

ISBN 978–1–4448–1833–8

Published by
F. A. Thorpe (Publishing)
Anstey, Leicestershire

Set by Words & Graphics Ltd.
Anstey, Leicestershire
Printed and bound in Great Britain by
T. J. International Ltd., Padstow, Cornwall

This book is printed on acid-free paper

To the memory of Frances Glynn

1

Mystery in Moon Lane

Manuscript found in the papers of Septimus Dacers, sometime detective in a private capacity. Mr Dacers was born in London in 1825 and died in that city in 1908, aged 83.

That evening and my unusual visitor have remained vivid in my memory down all the years and, through all the decades since, I have puzzled over the strange affair that followed his arrival at my apartments.

I was idle and worried in spite of the pleasant warmth of a late spring evening. The London authorities were worried, too, for the first cases of cholera had emerged among the ragged inhabitants of the wretched rookeries of the St. Giles region. It had not reached the dangerous proportions as it had among our unfortunate troops in the Crimea but it was likely to increase with the summer. My own trouble was money — or rather the lack of it. I needed a client, a commission to bring me out of idleness because I needed three weeks' back rent to take the angry glare from the eyes of my landlady, Mrs. Slingsby. That glare threatened eviction.

Sitting by the open window, gazing gloomily into the street, I was disturbed by a sharp tap at my door. Mrs. Slingsby's unmistakable calling card.

With a sinking heart, I opened the door and my landlady was indeed there. But she was not alone for, behind her stood a tall, gaunt man. Despite the warm evening, he was peculiarly muffled in a heavy black surcoat and with a scarf wrapped around the lower half of his face so that only a pair of glittering eyes showed between it and the brim of his tall hat.

'A gentleman to see you, Mr. Dacers,' said Mrs. Slingsby in an acid voice, which plainly had an undertone of: '*And you still owe three weeks' rent!*'

I thanked her, ushered in the visitor and hastily closed the door on the lady and her glare.

‘You are a detective, Mr. Dacers?’ the man spoke through his scarf. His accent was heavy and foreign.

I assured him that I was and waved him towards the better of my two shabby chairs.

‘But you are not associated with the police?’ he asked, seating himself.

‘No, I act in a private capacity but I have helped the police on occasion. I must warn you, though, that I never undertake anything contrary to criminal law,’ I told him.

‘I do not propose any illegal ventures,’ said my visitor, revealing that despite his heavy accent, his command of English was good. ‘But I do not want it known that I am here in London. I have come from France where I am known among the scientific community and there are those both here and in my home country who keenly seek intelligence of certain projects on which I am engaged.’

He began to unwind his concealing muffler, revealing a dark, sharply intelligent face with moustachios and beard of the fashion called an ‘imperial’.

‘My name is Duclois — Auguste Duclois. You might have heard of me,’ he declared somewhat in the manner of a grand actor.

‘Duclois, of the electrical impulses!’ I answered. ‘Yes, of course I’ve heard of you. Your name was in the papers not six months ago.’

He gave a snort. ‘The papers ridiculed me, M’sieu Dacers. They sneered at my experiments aimed at changing human behavior by electrical impulses. And all of them, in England, on the Continent and in America, had everything wrong, as usual. They didn’t understand the half of my reasoning. Damned ignorant scribblers, all of them!’

‘I’ve little knowledge of scientific matters,’ I said, noting that, with his erratic gestures of the arms and his rapid speech, my visitor was mounting what was obviously a hobbyhorse. Impatiently I waited for him to get to the point of his visit.

‘Ah, in that you are like most men, my dear sir,’ replied Duclois. ‘You can’t see an obvious fact when it is staring you in the face. It is given to genuine seers, such as myself, to grasp the potential of anything new on the scientific horizon. I haven't yet fully explored the possibilities of electricity but I know the wonders it can unfold, the untold benefits it can eventually bring to mankind. You might think we have reached the ultimate in progress now that we're in the great age of steam; that we have all but conquered the world with the huge engines seen so recently, grinding and clanking at your Great Exhibition of 1851 — but no! No, Mr. Dacers! There are more achievements to be aimed at. Consider the part the electric telegraph played in capturing that murderous couple, the Mannings, here in England only three or four years ago. But developments infinitely greater than the mere telegraph are waiting once we fully harness the mysteries of electricity. I am one of the select few who are engaged in that pursuit, sir, persevering despite the ridicule.'

'Would you care for a glass of sherry?' I

ventured, hoping he would refuse for my solitary bottle was all but down to the dregs.

'Thank you, no. I would prefer to get down to business. I am willing to hand over a ten guinea retainer here and now and a further ten on completion of a certain task.'

My heart lifted. The initial ten guineas alone would settle my rent bill and considerably replenish my supply of sherry, and twenty guineas all told for a single assignment was quite unprecedented.

I strove to put on the demeanor of a dignified man of business and said, soberly: 'As I am not at present engaged, sir, I can act on your behalf.'

'Tres bon!' he responded with a rare lapse into his native tongue. 'It is largely a matter of, as you might say here, keeping an eye on a certain person. I saw a newspaper report of your doing something similar in the recent railway fraud case in which the Metropolitan Police enlisted your help. That is why I sought you out.'

I shuddered, recalling the railway fraud case and the miserable winter hours I had spent watching certain premises and noting the comings and goings of various high-placed individuals and observing the companions they consorted with. Then the prospect of a twenty guinea fee brightened my mood again.

'I am on the brink of quite startling discoveries, notwithstanding the barbs of the scoffers,' continued Duclois. 'Not least among those scoffers is a great rival of mine, one who shuns the limelight so that few among his countrymen here in England even know his name. He is a man of ability for all his scoffing at fellow researchers and for all his deliberate choice of obscurity. I believe he is researching into the very revolutionary applications of electricity as I am myself. I want to know what he is up to, and I have a particular desire to know what equipment he is building and using.'

'But I'm no specialist in matters scientific,' I pointed out.

'It will be chiefly a matter of observation on your part, Mr. Dacers — well within your powers,' said Duclois. 'My wretched rival Amos Chaffin, this snake in the grass as you English say, has dogged me for years with his ridicule. He tried to make me a laughing stock at the Berlin Congress of Science in 1850, then went to ground here in London, going into obscurity to work on a scheme the very basis of which I know he stole from me. He doesn't know that I have followed him, and am aware of where he is lurking. I must know more, however, but dare not show myself to him.'

'Where might he be found?' I asked.

'Not far from here. He has established a workshop in a portion of an old warehouse in Moon Lane where he is working alone. Do you know Moon Lane?'

I nodded, flinching inwardly. It was dangerously close to the sprawling St. Giles slum, known to the criminal classes as 'The Holy Land'. Gangs of thieves and violent malefactors of every stripe inhabited it, clustering together in gangs to resist the forces of the law. Whenever the Peelers ventured there, they went in squads, often armed with cutlasses and sometimes pistols. However, the hefty fee promised by Monsieur Duclois was a powerful inducement.

'How will I know him?'

'Easily — a short, squat fellow, sharp-nosed and pockmarked. Oh, and he has a ridiculous set of false teeth which always seem to be in danger of falling out.'

'And what must I particularly note about Mr. Chaffin's activities?' I enquired.

'Particularly what materials are delivered to his place of experiment and in what quantity,' Duclois said. 'There will doubtless be carboys of acid and jars of distilled water and, very likely, sheets of slate. The scale of such deliveries will give me some idea of the scale of his experiments.'

'Merely that?' I asked.

'Not entirely. I suppose it will not be beyond your wit to enter his workshop and I greatly desire a sketch of what he is building there — the roughest sketch will do so long as you can indicate the size of whatever he has set up. Have you ever seen an electrical battery?'

'Yes, at the Great Exhibition in '51.'

'Well, I expect you'll see something of the kind at Chaffin's lair but probably on a very large scale, but I want to be sure. I must steal a march on the rogue — to pay him out for filching the foundations of my own plans, as I know he has. I want to forestall him in giving the world one of the most astonishing achievements known to science and to trounce him once and for all.' Duclois was gesticulating again. And his eyes were glittering with near fanaticism

'You have three days, Mr. Dacers. I shall be back then to discover your results. I shall not tell you where I am staying for it is essential that I remain as scarce as Chaffin himself while I'm in London.'

He fished inside his surcoat and produced a large purse from which he took a handful of gold sovereigns and silver. He counted out ten guineas and placed the money in my hand. 'And the rest on successful completion of the matter,' he said.

* * *

At once, I settled my back rent, which considerably sweetened Mrs. Slingsby's disposition and removed the threat of the debtors' prison. Next morning, I set about my commission, choosing the right moment to leave the house. It being Tuesday, Mrs. Slingsby sent her girl slavey out to the market as usual then departed on her regular weekly visit to her sister so I was alone in the house. I put on rough boots, moleskin trousers, a coarse jacket and a stove-in hat such as a workingman might wear, a costume suited to an excursion in the region of The Holy Land. I applied a scrubby set of whiskers and false moustaches, put a small notebook and a blacklead pencil into my pocket and went forth. I left the house by the rear door and, after walking the back lanes of several streets, I emerged in the region of Oxford Street.

The air was balmy and the odors of the streets were only too evident. In the better class thoroughfares, workmen were spreading quicklime in the gutters, following the usual precaution in the cholera season. I walked along Oxford Street, heading for the vicinity of St. Giles, trying to think up some stratagem for entering the Moon Lane warehouse.

Midway along Oxford Street, I passed a workman, shoveling quicklime and hoarsely croaking a song that was all the rage that year of 1855:

'Not long ago, in Vestminster,
There lived a ratcatcher's daughter;
But she din't quite live in Vestminster,
For she lived t'other side of the vater . . .'

Ratcatcher! I thought to myself, *Now, that's the kind of man who might find employment in the region of Moon Lane.* I also took note of the raffish singer's Cockney idiom as a pointer to character.

Moon Lane was every bit as unprepossessing as it ever was. It was a narrow, snaking crack between old, gray, frowning warehouse buildings most of which seemed to be empty. Its slimy cobbles were broken and there was a liberal scattering of puddles of filth underfoot.

No human life was in evidence at first. Then, just as I entered the lane, a heavy cart drawn by two horses trundled out of a yard set one side of one of the buildings. The driver was a surly looking fellow, smoking a clay pipe and with a dirty sack as a cloak. I had to squeeze hard against a cracked wall to allow the animals and the vehicle to pass me. The carter considered me with a beery eye.

'Vot cheer, mate?' he growled as he passed, which encouraged me to believe my disguise was convincing.

'Vot cheer?' I replied. 'Votcher been deliverin' — best ale and porter?'

'My eye! Nuffin' so bloomin' prime as that, vorse luck,' he called over his shoulder. 'Four carboys of bloomin' acid. Fine bloomin' boozin' that'd make!'

As the cart rumbled past, I took note of the legend on its side: 'Alfred Musprat and Sons, Suppliers of chemicals and acids, Cheapside.'

Four carboys of acid. This was a good start and this yard was obviously attached to the building, which Amos Chaffin had made his base of operations. I stood at the gate of the yard and surveyed it. Like everything about Moon Lane, it was gloomy and mean. Surrounded on three sides by the flaking walls of neighboring warehouses, it was cluttered with rubbish. The doors of the surrounding buildings were closed and some were boarded up. One, however, stood open, the only sign of there being any kind of activity in the place. I could see four carboys lined up just inside the doorway

I ventured into the yard and looked about cautiously. It was quiet with no sign of life. Cautiously, I walked towards the open door and entered a damp and musty, windowless corridor, shrouded in gloom. Again, there was no sign of anyone but the carboys of acid deposited on the threshold suggested that there might be some form of occupancy.

To one side of the corridor, there was another open door and I entered it. I was in a large room where, against one wall, stood four square glass containers, taller than myself, and each filled with a liquid. Within them, I also saw what looked like slabs of slate. I recalled what Auguste

Duclois had said about electric batteries and saw that they did resemble those seen at the Great Exhibition but built on a far bigger scale. There was also a large board with a tangle of wires on it as well as a metal lever on something of the pattern of those in railway signal boxes.

So far, everything had gone swimmingly. I had not encountered any obstruction and I could begin sketching what I had discovered. Producing my notebook and blacklead pencil, I drew to the best of my ability the set of large containers, the board and the lever.

Then I heard a footfall in a far corner of the gloomy room, looked towards it and quickly whipped my notebook behind my back as I saw a man of short stature emerging from a door, which the shadows had all but hidden.

'Who the devil are you? What are you doing here?' he bellowed as he advanced on me. He had on a slop coat such as those worn by all manner of workers to protect their everyday street clothes, and a tall hat. True to the description of Duclois, his nose was sharp and his face crabbed and angry.

'Who are you, damn you?' he demanded again and he quickly put a hand to his mouth, obviously to secure dentures which his angry spluttering seemed to have shaken loose.

I kept my notebook behind my back and began to brazen it out. 'Rats, sir. I'm on the look out for rats,' I said.

'Rats? I have not sought the services of a ratcatcher,' bellowed the man who was very clearly Amos Chaffin. 'You're trespassing! Who are you?'

'Smith, sir — Jem Smith. I'm just doin' my job as instructed by my guv'nor,' I lied, turning on my Cockney persona.

Chaffin squinted at me with an eye matching that of Auguste Duclois for fanatical glitter. 'Governor? Who's your governor?'

'Mr. George Nobbs, practical ratcatcher, from over Seven Dials vay. It vos the cove owning that warehouse over yonder,' I waved vaguely towards the yard beyond the building, 'vot asked him to look into the matter of rats seen on his premises. 'Go and look over the job, Jem,' says Mr. Nobbs, as he often does. Having some notion of how many rats and where they're nesting helps us sort out vot we needs in the vay of traps and poisons, d'you see, sir. Have you seen any rats about?'

'Of course I have,' sputtered Amos Chaffin, adjusting his false teeth again. 'Rats are always everywhere in London. And I put up with them without the services of ratcatchers.'

'You'll pardon me, sir, but that's a mistake,' I said. 'There's talk that the cholera is spread by rats. They're highly dangerous, sir.'

'Indeed!' growled Chaffin. 'I heard there's a theory that it's spread by bad water.'

'All wrong, sir. It's rats vot spread it. You have to root 'em out. Have to find their nests and destroy 'em. I couldn't help noticin' that there's perfect nestin' conditions behind all that odd stuff you have up against that vall.' I indicated the equipment associated with his experimenting.

His eyes flashed and his teeth threatened to jump out of his mouth of their own volition. 'Odd stuff!' he howled. 'Do you know what that equipment is? Do you know what you're in the presence of — what epoch-making scientific advances are in the making in this very room, Smith?'

I shrugged and answered: 'I'm sure I dunno, sir. I ain't had the schoolin' to understand science. I reckon most of it is gammon.'

'Gammon! You call scientific investigation gammon?' he exploded. 'Why, man, here in this very place, miracles are about to be performed upon any objects or persons placed within the electrical field of my machine. Only this morning I concluded calculations which will have far reaching results — results hitherto undreamed of, even by a fool of a Frog named Duclois who is the bane of my existence.'

I was beginning to think that both Duclois and Chaffin must be totally mad.

It was at this point, with Chaffin in such close proximity to me, that I dropped the notebook that I had been concealing behind my back all the time.

Sod's law decreed that it landed on the grimy floor wide open, with my rough sketches fully visible and Chaffin saw them.

He gave a howl. 'Sketches, by God! You've been sketching my equipment! You're no ratcatcher — you're a damnable spy! You're employed by Duclois, I'll warrant!' He made a dive for the book, but I, being younger and more agile, reached it first. As I stowed it in my pocket, he grappled with me, clutching the lapels of my jacket.

'Give me that book, you scoundrel!' he snarled.

Locked together, we reeled across the room, grunting and clawing at each other. Then, near the glass containers and the lever, we fell over and smote the lever with the combined weight of our two bodies. It creaked over from the upright position as the two of us went sprawling, still struggling. It seemed to me that we fell into something like a tunnel, to the accompaniment of a thundering and rushing confusion of sound and I was dimly aware that Chaffin was there with me, going through the same experience. Then came an abrupt stop to the falling and I was lying on the ground in what I believed was the same warehouse building.

It was dark and, somewhere in the darkness, I heard the voice of Amos Chaffin shout something incomprehensible that was at once drowned out by more noise — such noise as I never before heard. It was a crashing and banging and thundering of loud explosions and a constant, thrumming droning sound. Then the whole warehouse shook under a dull, shuddering reverberation and there was suddenly light behind us, the blazing yellow and crimson flickering of flames. It briefly illumined the grotesque form of Chaffin in his slop coat and tall hat, running away from where I lay — presumably to escape the flames that were threatening us.

He had barely covered a few yards when a rafter came crashing down on him from the roof. I somehow got to my feet and, in a chaotic welter of swirling smoke and dust, tried to stagger towards where I last saw Chaffin, hoping to help him. I made hardly any progress because I could only blunder around, coughing and half blinded in the confusion.

Then dimly, in this hellish nightmare, I heard a man's urgent voice shouting something like: '*Here — Harry, Nobby, Jack — get the hoses over on this side — there seems to be a bloke trapped under a rafter . . . quick about it . . . alert the Rescue . . .*' Before I realized it, I had somehow wandered free of the building which was no longer a building but a tumbled mass of bricks, just visible through a swirl of smoke and flames.

Holding my hands against my ears and trying to clear my throat of smoke and dust, I staggered across broken cobbles and shattered bricks, found the doorway of a building and plunged into it, seeking cover and trying to recover my breath. Out of the confusion, came a man in a strange costume, though I recognized his greatcoat as something like a Peeler's. He had an odd helmet like an upturned pudding basin and made of metal. Sure enough, though, the word *Police* was painted on it in white capitals. His face was smudged with black marks and, like myself, he was choking in the smoke. Coughing, he joined me, leaning against the closed door.

'Hello, mate. You all right?' he shouted over the din when he found his breath. He looked at me enquiringly in the dancing light of the flames, and grinned.

'Cor! Where've you come from in that get-up — out of a pantomime? That battered old topper of yours is no protection in this lot. You want to watch out for your head and there's a cut on your face. There's a first-aid post a bit down the lane. Go and ask 'em to clean it up for you.'

He slipped away into the smoky, blazing chaos, leaving me more bewildered than before.

Now that my head had cleared, I remembered Amos Chaffin, trapped under a rafter in the warehouse. I had to get back to him — had to help him out. I was beginning to see that our predicament had something to do with his electrical equipment, which our grappling must have accidentally activated. I recalled what Chaffin had said

— something about objects or people being affected by the electrical field of his machine.

Though I was no scientist, it seemed to me that if I was to get back to where I belonged, I had to be within the influence of that field, which lay somewhere within the warehouse.

Crouching into the smoke and flames, I scrambled over humps of rubble towards the wreckage of the warehouse on which the men in the strange costumes and metal helmets were playing jets of water on to the flames. I got within a section of shattered wall and blundered onward until I believed I was somewhere near where I last saw Chaffin. Then I heard a hoarse voice, yelling above the explosive cacophony: '*Hey, come back! You can't go in there! What're you up to — looting? Come back, dammit — come back . . .* '

The agitated voice thinned, became distant then merged into that same whirling, rushing sound which had accompanied the fall through the tunnel and, indeed, I was falling through the tunnel again, being whelmed breathlessly away into darkness.

* * *

'How are you feeling now, my good man?' asked the man in the frock coat who seemed to appear out of nowhere. 'You've taken a bad turn, but at least, it's not the cholera.'

I was sitting in a chair and the elderly man in the frock coat was hovering over me. I saw a woman in a white cap and with a white apron over her crinoline go past. At least, I was in surroundings I understood, away from nightmarish explosions, fires and men in grotesque clothing, struggling against a hellish background.

'Where . . . ' I started.

'Where are you?' finished the elderly man. 'Why in the St. Giles Cholera Hospital, where we're doing the best we can in this awful epidemic. A charitable gentleman saw you staggering in the street near Moon Lane, thought at first you had been imbibing then felt you had fallen victim to the cholera. He put you in his carriage and brought you here. I'm a doctor and you plainly haven't caught the disease, though you've been here the better part of the day, delirious and mumbling. There's no sign of any drink on you, but you look as if you've had a hard time of it. Not been attacked by one of those street ruffians, have you? You have a cut on your face which we dressed with a strip of court plaster and generally cleaned you up.'

I felt my face and discovered that my false beard and moustaches had somehow become lost. I was still in my disguise as a workingman and hoped that was what the doctor took me for. I assured him I had recovered and was able to make my way home and he, kindly man, fortified me with a glass of brandy and water before allowing me to leave.

For a couple of days, I kept to my rooms, recovering my strength and wondering about the strange and alarming bout of delirium I had endured. But was it really delirium?

I kept an eye on the papers and on the second day, saw a paragraph stating that the landlord of a set of warehouses in Moon Lane was seeking one of his tenants who had unaccountably gone missing. He was a Mr. Chaffin, a gentleman of reclusive nature who was apparently engaged on some kind of scientific research.

And of M. Auguste Duclois I had no word. He did not appear on the appointed day to pay me the remainder of my fee, but then I had hardly earned it.

A week after my strange experience, the ever-helpful newspapers gave me startling information. It concerned the fatal explosion of the boilers of the steam packet Lily of France en route to Dieppe, one of the shocking tragedies of 1855. Among the list of dead passengers was the name of M. Auguste Duclois, known for his somewhat eccentric contributions to scientific studies.

This gave me pause. It looked as if he was hastily departing the shores of England. Could it be that, alerted by news of the search for Amos Chaffin, he took fright thinking that someone who knew of his bitter opposition to Chaffin might go to the police with the suggestion that he had something to do with the disappearance?

Hoping that if anyone saw a youngish man in rough clothing and with a scrubby beard and moustaches entering the warehouse in Moon Lane just before Chaffin's disappearance they would not identify him as myself, I lay low for a spell.

I hoped, too, that the next client to come along would be as liberal with his funds as the much-lamented M. Auguste Duclois.

* * *

Extract from a letter written in 1965 by Mr. Kenneth Spence to his friend Mr. Jim Morton. Mr. Spence, a retired Chief Superintendent of the Metropolitan Police, died four years later. He joined the police service in 1922 and retired in 1952. During the London blitz of 1940 onwards, as an Inspector, he had charge of a large portion of central London, coordinating operations between the police and the various branches of the

Civil Defense services.

Mr. Morton was his lifelong friend from schooldays. Although a chartered accountant by profession, during the second world war, he was a Column Officer in the Auxiliary Fire Service and by coincidence, carried out his duties in the area of London covered by Inspector Spence Mr. Morton died in 1973.

Dear Jim,

A couple of letters ago, you mentioned that strange affair of the corpse in old-fashioned clothing taken from a burning building in Moon Lane by your chaps and the rescue people during the Blitz at Christmas 1940. You'll remember how his get-up made us think at first that he might have come from some panto or Dickensian show but, by then, the Blitz had reached such intensity that even the bravest of brave showbiz people had closed up shop. A story went about that someone else in antique clothing was seen in the region and one of my bobbies swore he'd met him and spoken to him while both were sheltering in a doorway. He even gave me a description of him but he was never traced. Ever afterwards, the PC claimed he'd met a ghost.

You'll no doubt remember Moon Lane. It was all but falling in when Goering's people flew over to demolish it. All that area of London was razed and redeveloped by London County Council long before but Moon Lane somehow lingered on though it was scheduled to be demolished when the war stopped all slum clearance. Such a place might well be haunted.

As for that corpse, many aspects of it were truly odd and I don't think I ever told you about all of them. You'll remember dropping me a private note, saying you found his costume and sidewhiskers and everything else about him strange. Because of the pressures of the Blitz, we could not hold inquests and burial was usually quick and without real investigation but your note caused me to drop in at the emergency mortuary to see the body. As you told me, he was a middle-aged man, pockmarked and, even naked as he was when I saw him, he looked distinctly old-fashioned.

I was lucky in that old Jock McAllen was in charge of the mortuary. He was a veteran pathologist who came out of retirement to help in the emergency. He'd had an unusual career, starting out in dentistry then changing to surgery. However, he kept up an interest in the history of dentistry and had written a book on it.

Looking over the body with me, he said he was baffled by the fact that all the clothing was of a style around a century before. He even had antique underwear. A couple of Queen Victoria sovereigns and some pennies and silver, all dated around the 1840s and 1850s were found in his trousers pocket and Jock kept them to hand over to the police.

'You'll notice his pockmarks,' said Jock. 'That was typical in the middle of the last century. Smallpox was common and a great many people recovered from it but were marked for life. But it's the teeth — those false teeth — that intrigue me. There's no doubt, Inspector Spence, that they're Waterloo teeth!'

I asked what Waterloo teeth were and he told me that, when creating false teeth was an imperfect art, there was a demand for real teeth to be used — sound teeth from young corpses. Because so many soldiers of all sides killed at Waterloo in 1815 were mere youths, there was afterwards a wholesale digging up of corpses and 'Waterloo teeth' were manufactured all over Britain, France and Belgium. Old Jock said that, even late in the century, people were chewing with the teeth of young men killed in 1815.

'A man of 1940', said old Jock, 'might deck himself out in the full costume of the 19th Century and, by coincidence, even be heavily pockmarked, Inspector, but is he likely to wear a set of Waterloo teeth, even if he inherited them from his great grandfather? Frankly, I'm totally bewildered.'

And so am I, Jim. I've been

bewildered all these years. It was as if the man had been somehow transported from the middle of the 19th Century to the thick of our turmoil in 1940. But that is utterly impossible. Well, it is. Isn't it . . . ?

2

The Model

'My father knew him, you know,' said George Fennister. 'In fact, they were pretty close towards the end of Costigan's life. They were in the same platoon in the army, thrown together by sheer chance: my father, the aspiring art historian and Costigan, the rising young painter. My father never forgot how he met his end one night in 1917. Costigan was sent out with a wire party and the Germans opened up with heavy artillery while they were in no-man's land. Nothing was ever seen of them again. Probably, they were just blown to bits. That was the way of things in that war.'

The old man shrugged and pushed a faded brown envelope across the table towards me. 'Half a dozen photos my father left. You'll spot Costigan, of course. My daughter's had enhanced copies made for her family album, so you can have these. They're a bit battered but they might be useful for your book.'

I opened the envelope eagerly, reflecting on the generosity of the old gallery owner in so willingly parting with these precious relics of this long dead father. They were indeed battered but clear enough, sepia visions of young soldiers of First World War vintage, acting the fool in some obscure French village behind the line. They were cavorting with the desperate merriment common to that generation of unwilling citizen-soldier, so obviously aware that every next minute might easily be their last one.

'My father's the one with the little moustache which he hoped would grow into an impressive military one — if he was spared,' commented Mr. Fennister. 'You'll recognize Costigan easily enough.'

I did. There he was, Fred Costigan, the unpredictable wild man of the pre-1914 art world, looking astonishingly boyish and vulnerable without the famous beard. In one picture, he was grinning, waving his steel helmet in the air. In another, he held a wine bottle to his lips, as if trying to capture an echo of the roaring nights he drank away with the bohemian set of Camden Town.

'They're wonderful, Mr. Fennister,' I said. 'I'm so grateful to you. They'll help towards the human picture of Costigan I hope to give, showing him as something more than an arrogant drunkard.'

'My father considered his wild behavior to be mostly an act,' replied George Fennister. 'He had a softer side which he tried to keep hidden. He was once madly in love but there was a row and the girl disappeared before they could make it up and Costigan became morose. When the Great War started, he enlisted very early, probably to escape a life which had become pretty empty and his remarkable early promise as a painter was failing to flower. He somehow survived in the trenches until as late as 1917.'

'The girl?' I asked. 'She would be the unknown model whom he painted? They rowed over heaven knows what and Costigan destroyed the picture.'

'It sounds as if you've been reading

McArdle's book on Costigan, written in the twenties, Mr. Jevons.' Fennister gave a tolerant smile.

'Of course, it's the only available source — but it's badly flawed. McArdle made a big thing about knowing Costigan, but the truth is he hardly knew him. They moved in different circles and were associated with different art schools. McArdle was at the Slade while, as you know, Costigan was at Readly's, where you are. They had only a slight acquaintance. McArdle was a hack on the make.'

He rose from his chair, looked at me levelly and said: 'You know, I like you, Mr. Jevons, and I admire your work as a painter. I'm pleased to know you are trying to produce a decent book on Costigan. He deserves some proper treatment, even at this late date. Now that we've met face-to-face, I can see you are genuinely interested in the subject. The fact is, I have some rare relics of Costigan, which I've hung on to ever since my father's death. One, indeed, is of enormous interest. Now that I'm leaving London for good, I have a mind to give them to you. I think they'll open doors for you in your research.'

'Relics of Costigan and you're giving them to me?' I said. 'But they must be valuable. You can get a good price for them.'

The old man shook his head. 'What, from some rich collector who'll just let them gather more dust? No, I'm not badly off for money after sixty years in the top bracket of the art game. They'll be better off in your hands. Come with me.'

He led me from the small room at the rear of the gallery which he was soon to sell up, took me to a back stairway tucked away behind his main showroom and we climbed its creaking and uncarpeted treads.

'You see,' said the dealer as we went, 'Costigan must have had a premonition about his death because he made a will bequeathing certain property to my father, probably feeling that, as a man who was interested in art history, he would appreciate them. There are some papers, which will help you. For instance, a few minutes ago, you spoke of the girl he painted as 'an unknown model', because you relied on McArdle. But, as you'll see, she was not unknown. Her name was Katherine Cranshaw and he was certainly in love with her.'

We reached a narrow landing and he opened a door. Beyond it was a dusty attic, cluttered with old furniture. In a corner, stood an easel with a cloth covering what was obviously a canvas positioned on it.

'Now, here's a rough diary kept by Costigan,' George Fennister said, opening a drawer in a scarred wooden table. The booklet he handed me was tattered, stained and dog-eared. I grasped it eagerly, hardly able to credit my good luck. I had placed an advertisement in an art magazine saying I was researching a book on Costigan and sought contact with anyone who might have helpful material. George Fennister was the only person to reply and I never imagined that, on this visit to his gallery, I would encounter a treasure trove.

'This is wonderful,' I said as I leafed quickly through the book, finding page after stained page of penciled handwriting, frequently soiled by what I felt might be the end of the Western Front. 'Something on Costigan's life in his own hand is stunning.'

'It might well help in remedying the false impressions which McArdle perpetrated,' said George Fennister. 'One of them being something you said only a few minutes ago: that Costigan destroyed the painting of Katherine after he fell out with her. Well, the truth is he didn't. He had wished to make the painting his masterpiece — as you'll see from his notes. He really wanted to capture her beauty and put it before all the world. After he rowed with her and after a heavy drinking session, he soured on the girl and on his own ability. He felt he had not done justice to her beauty and, anyway, he believed he hated her — but that was only a passing notion, fired by his drunken stupidity. He did not wholly destroy the painting however. He loaded a brush with black paint and what he did was — this . . .'

He moved quickly over the dusty floor

of the attic to the covered painting on its easel. He took a corner of the covering, whipped it off the canvas and I gasped at what was revealed.

It was a full-length nude, a young woman, painted with such sensitivity that I felt I was looking on living flesh. She had her back to the viewer and her head was turned so that she was looking over her shoulder out of the picture — at least she would have been looking if she had a face.

All her facial features had been obliterated by a series of thick lines of black paint, crisscrossed on the canvas as if it had been attacked by a frenzied vandal. There was absolutely no trace of the facial beauty that must surely have matched the vibrant, young womanly body the artist had depicted.

'You mean, this is it?' I gasped. 'This is the very picture which Costigan painted — the one McArdle claimed was destroyed? But, yes, it must be. I recognize his style, his brushwork.'

'It's the very one,' George Fennister confirmed. 'He slashed paint all over her face, then regretted it. He stored the canvas with his other belongings when he went off to the war. As you'll see from his diary, he hoped to return, make it up with Katherine and repair the damage by really doing justice to her beauty. It was a dream which kept him going through all those wretched months in the trenches.'

The old man paused, shook his head and sighed. 'But it wasn't to be. Soon after he enlisted, Katherine simply disappeared. His diary records show he searched for her on his few brief leaves, all to no avail. In the end, the war swallowed him up. He left the painting to my father with his other mementos and my father hung on to them. He concentrated on building up his gallery and dealership after the war and never entered into the controversies of the art world, although he could have corrected much of the misinformation put about by McArdle through his ill-informed book. Anyway, perhaps you can do it all these years on, Mr. Jevons. I'm selling up but I've kept this painting out of my stock-in-trade. You may have it with all the other Costigan items.'

I was astounded by his generosity. 'But, defaced though it is, it's surely valuable just because it's a Costigan.'

George Fennister shrugged. 'No matter. I'm not exactly struggling for money and the painting might assist you in your work. It might help you towards a balanced view of Costigan and I know my father would have appreciated it. For all his wildness, Costigan was his good friend and a reliable comrade in the horrors of the Western Front. The diary does give one some understanding of the real Costigan. Under his pose as a drunken Bohemian, he was remarkably strait-laced. There was the matter of his row with Katherine, for instance. It was brought on by his stuffy attitude.'

'I thought the cause was unknown. McArdle says they quarrelled for some unknown reason,' I said.

Fennister chuckled. 'That was McArdle all over. He cobbled together the so-called life of Costigan without any real facts. Well, the diary will show you that they rowed over a tattoo.'

'A tattoo?'

'Yes. It seems Katherine tried to be as unconventional as Costigan made himself out to be and she had herself tattooed, something a young woman hardly ever did in those days. She had his name, 'Fred' tattooed on her shoulder and it caused Costigan to hit the ceiling. His essential fastidiousness came into play. He liked a woman to be totally feminine and he claimed Katherine was defiling herself with the tattoo. He said only rough characters like sailors and navvies went in for tattoos. Furthermore, he'd always despised the name Fred and he was annoyed at her marking herself for life with it. Tattoos couldn't be removed in those days, remember.'

I left Fennister's premises elated and enlightened, with the precious diary in my pocket and the defaced picture of the beauty which Costigan had wanted to put before the world under my arm still covered by its cloth. The art dealer had not only exploded my belief in McArdle's work, hitherto regarded as the most reliable outline of the young life of Fred Costigan, he had presented me with material that was absolutely invaluable.

My car was parked in front of the gallery and as I was carefully slanting the large canvas across the rear seat, a corner of the covering slipped, revealing the back of the painting and I saw something penciled on the bottom of the wooden stretcher. I read:

'F. Costigan. Readly's School of Fine Art, London, WC1, February 1914.'

So, I mused, could it be that Costigan had tackled his attempt at his masterpiece at the very school of which both of us were graduates and where we both eked out our painting careers with part-time tutorships? I had imagined that he worked on it in his studio near Mornington Crescent but perhaps, like myself, he managed to put in some personal work while engaged with students in the very life rooms in which I was employed.

Readly's dated from the 1870's and its layout had hardly changed over the many decades. I knew that the life rooms had been used in that capacity since the creation of the school and, like myself, Costigan had tutored in advanced painting from life in them. I looked at the penciled date again: 'February 1914'. I remembered that the First Great War broke out in the August of that year and that Costigan had enlisted very early as one of the great rush of young men eager to take up arms. Probably, this attempt to catch the beauty of an obscure girl who would totally disappear from ken was the very last significant work of a young man who was also destined to be obliterated.

The poignancy of it was brought home to me as, back in my flat, I read Costigan's diary far into the night. From faded words, penciled on grubby pages, perhaps written when huddled against the sandbags of a trench or when snatching some respite in a rest station in an estaminet, in some cruelly battered French village, I absorbed Fred Costigan's remorse and hopes. He cursed himself for a fool for parting so bitterly from the only woman who really meant anything to him.

The more I read, the more I formed a

new picture of Costigan. I saw how the received view of him, based almost wholly on McArdle's book, was wrong. He was far more than a rowdy young drunkard who nevertheless had a rare artistic gift that the brutality of war blotted out. It was as if I was hearing his voice from the cauldron of the dreadful conflict that engulfed the world early in the Twentieth Century.

It spoke of one who was so obviously the true Fred Costigan, a sensitive man who longed to be free of the lunacy of wholesale slaughter to find his lost love and place her beauty before the world through the art his brain and fingers longed to practice. Years before, I became fascinated by this young man because of the slender body of work he left behind. As a working artist myself, I found an affinity with him which I could not fully understand. I determined to attempt a new biography of him to update the out-of-print one of McArdle.

Now, thanks to the dog-eared diary, the task had become imperative. I felt I owed a debt to this man who had perished on a battlefield of long ago.

From that tattered record, I learned how, on his few meager leaves in London, he tried without success to find his missing love and nostalgic yearnings for the days that used to be leapt off the pages.

'We had a respite last week and rested in a small café. I fell in with some of the South Lancashires who shared the line with us. One had an old gramophone and a solitary record, which he played over and over again. It was that silly ragtime item to which Katherine and I danced many times and which we sang together with abandon:

'I'll make you my own
In our own little home.
My madtime, gladtime,
Ragtime girl.'

'The words were banal and ridiculous but they brought back those nights before the war. I could not rid my mind of the memory of Katherine for days. I longed to be with her again and enjoy the silly moments of singing that song with her. And mingled with it all was my regret at rowing with her and spoiling the picture of her which I had so much wanted to make my masterpiece.'

Costigan's diary ended on a date in 1917 with a terse entry:

'Going up the line tomorrow. Rumors of a big push.'

The remainder of the little book contained only blank pages, which told their own ominous tale.

During a long night of reading interspersed with sessions of studying the canvas I had propped against a wall, considering Costigan's spoiled masterpiece, I formed distinctly sympathetic feelings for him. Artistic London in the days before the Great War knew him as a roaring Bohemian. But I had encountered a sensitive man, a man in love who regretted that his impetuous temper led to his mauling the highly accomplished attempt to put his lost love's beauty before the world. I stared at the brutal black lines he had slashed across the face of the girl and I longed to see the beauty that had been so deliberately obliterated.

Next morning, I set off for the school with Costigan and the lost Katherine haunting me. We were in the midst of the summer school sessions and I was mixing my regular work with four days a week instructing in advanced life painting, all easy enough because the summer school attracted competent students, many of whom were professionals seeking added experience of working from models.

Because such students required only a modicum of advice now and again, I had hardly any teaching to do and could devote some time to personal projects. I usually did so from a model of my own choice rather than the one posed in the center of the life room and I worked in a curtained-off area to one side of the major studio.

Looking back on events of the days following my evening with Costigan's diary, they seem to be shrouded in a kind of haze, as if they occurred when I was in a dream-state. I went into the school that morning knowing that my class had been comfortably set up over the previous few days, working under its own steam from one of our regular pool of models. At that stage, I could begin some work of my own and, though I had a good-sized canvas already primed, I had not selected a model. I had a vague idea of doing a female nude study and it now seems that the notion was prompted from outside of myself while I was in the hazy condition that I believe overcame me the moment I entered the school.

Looking in at the office on the ground floor, I asked Margaret, the general factotum, if I might have a model.

'June has already gone up to your studio as usual,' she said, meaning the regular model from whom my class was working.

'I don't mean June. I mean a model for some work of my own.'

'Sorry, I'm afraid there isn't a spare model. You know how things are at summer school time,' Margaret replied. 'If a girl comes in, I'll send her up.'

Disgruntled, I went upstairs. The corridor off which the life studios were situated was empty save for a solitary woman walking ahead of me. She was tall, slender, dark-haired and wearing a dressing gown. She was bare-legged and barefoot, presenting an appearance which, in any art school indicates a life model. She turned a sharp corner ahead of me but when I turned it, she had disappeared with what seemed remarkable rapidity.

Puzzled and experiencing that strange haziness, I entered the studio where my class was established. June, the model, was already in her agreed pose and the class, eager in its early start, as ever with summer school classes, was keenly at work.

'Good morning. Everyone happy with what they are doing?' I asked, attempting some morning breeziness. A chorus of satisfied 'Good mornings' came from behind the easels and nobody demanded my time.

In my curtained-off area, I found a tall, dark-haired girl, unclothed and standing still on the small podium as if in a prearranged pose.

Her back was to the prepared canvas I

had placed on my easel the previous day. In the mental fogginess that imparted a feeling of unreality, I walked to the easel and the girl looked over her shoulder, smiled at me and said: 'Good morning Mr. Jevons. I think this is how you want me posed, isn't it?'

I nodded and noted the dressing gown lying on a chair and, in that same fogged way, realized that she was the girl who had walked ahead of me in the corridor, yet I could not understand how she came to be in my portion of the studio. The whole time factor made it impossible for her to be one of the regular rota of models who had reported at the office and whom Margaret had sent upstairs. Then there was the strange matter of her taking up a pose of her own accord and my unquestioning acceptance of it. Curiously, I had little desire to question her though I made a half-hearted attempt.

'I haven't seen you about before, have I?'

'Oh, I've been around for some time,' she said, smiling over her shoulder, where upon my questioning ceased for I saw she was stunningly beautiful with huge, dark and liquid eyes and a slender, entrancingly formed body. I knew only an overwhelming desire to capture her on canvas, so I hastily put on my smock and set about preparing a palette.

How best can I describe my actions for the bulk of that day except by saying I painted? I painted as I had never painted before, all the time enveloped in that peculiar mental fog and scarcely conscious of my surroundings. Looking back, I have only a vague recollection of preparing the preliminary sketch of the girl who stood motionless on the podium, a perfect model in her pose and her ability to remain totally still. Then I plunged into the work of painting with a vigor alien to my usual painstaking approach.

There was no conversation between us. None seemed necessary and I had no indication to make lighthearted chat as a means of easing the strain of her task. I worked with a positive passion, oblivious to everything but the driven desire to portray the girl with her classic beauty and her half-saucy, half-innocent smile as she looked over her shoulder at me.

I have recollections of now and again suggesting she rested while I ventured out of my nook and made what was really a token circuit of the students working from the model in the larger studio, giving a suggestion here and there, answering an occasional query and ensuring that June, their model, had her proper rest breaks. When I returned to my own curtained-off corner, my model was always there, standing on the podium, posed correctly and needing no repositioning.

Then I would hurl myself once more into what had now almost become the be-all and end-all of my existence: the striving for perfection in placing of this girl's image on canvas. It went on all that day and I was scarcely aware of anything but the work in hand. Absorbed in the task, I was unaware of my surroundings though, now and again, from the street outside, I heard the clatter of horses' hooves, the trundling of iron-rimmed cartwheels, the occasional honking of a motor-horn and once, the hoarse voice of a newsboy shouting the afternoon edition:

'*Evening News! Evening News!* Mr. Asquith's important speech in the House! Important statement by the Prime Minister . . . '

Late in the afternoon, the bell marking the close of lessons clanged through the corridors and I emerged from what I suppose must have been a frenzy of painting, gasping like a swimmer coming up for air. I moved to one side to begin cleaning my brushes and, all at once, realized that the girl was no longer there. Nor was her robe. Somehow, without my seeing or hearing her move, she had simply disappeared.

For a moment, I stood as if paralyzed, gazing at the vacant podium, then I gathered my wits and stepped out of my curtained-off corner. In the main body of the studio, my students were gathering their gear, most preparing to go down to the evening lecture, a regular feature of the summer school.

'Did anyone see my model go out of

here a moment or two ago?' I asked, to be met with blank stares all round.

'A tall girl, slim, with dark hair,' I persisted.

'I didn't realize you had a model in there, Ted,' responded one. 'I thought you were doing some private work without a model.'

'Well, I looked in quickly to ask your advice, Mr. Jevons,' said another, a middle-aged woman who seemed in awe of me and always addressed me formally. 'But I didn't bother when I saw the way you were and I didn't notice any model.'

'What do you mean by the way I was?'

She shuffled her feet awkwardly. 'Well, you were concentrating very deeply on your painting and — sort of — well, grunting and muttering as you worked. I didn't think it was right to disturb you. I'm certain I didn't see a model, though.'

I watched the students file out of the door aware of one or two shooting me a dubious parting glance then, with the studio cleared, I made a half-hearted tour of the room, thinking I might come across the girl, hiding as some sort of silly joke.

Deep down, however, I knew I was not going to find her. She had gone as quickly and mysteriously as she had earlier appeared in front of me in the corridor.

I left the school in a state of mind I find hard to describe. I was not quite in the haze that seemed to envelope me through the day but still not appreciating my surroundings with normal clarity and lucidity. I supposed I was simply tired through the intense exertions of the day and, on reaching my flat I had a quick bite to eat and turned in. In no time, I fell into a deep sleep.

Once, I awakened, suddenly recalling the sound of hooves in the street outside the studio window and the voice of the newspaper vendor and questions hammered at my brain:

When was the constant clatter of horses last heard as a regular part of London street noise? When did a newspaper boy last call his wares in a London street? Come to that, when was such a thing as a newsboy last seen?

Certainly not in my time. And what was he shouting? Something about the

Prime Minister and his statement. And the Prime Minister's name — Mr. Asquith! What did I know of Asquith? Not much except that he was Premier when the First World War started and was eventually replaced by Lloyd George . . . all well before my time . . . long, long before my time . . .

I drifted into sleep once more and woke refreshed and eager for work.

Curiously, the questions of the night hardly surfaced as I breakfasted briefly and hastened back to the school.

Some inner conviction told me I should find the model waiting in my curtained-off cubbyhole and so she was. After hastily greeting my students and making a cursory check of their progress with a few words of advice or encouragement here and there, I found the girl already perfectly posed on the podium.

I suppose my greeting was almost offhand because I was so consumed by a desire to be working on the canvas. She replied with a beaming smile over her shoulder as she held the backward looking pose and I plunged at the work, deeply and intensely striving to render as much a living likeness of that perfect feminine form as I could. There was no question of my talking to the girl; no curiosity concerning how she came there or from whence she came. I wanted only to work and I was soon deeply absorbed — and hearing again, dimly, the clopping of hooves and the occasional note of a motor horn, which I knew was created by an antiquated instrument, the kind in which a rubber bulb was squeezed in the hand. None of it mattered. My only consideration was finishing this painting.

I finished with what must have been record speed after a day in which I had no concept of time. I now have no recollection of taking a break for a meal or even, in defiance of the school's regulations, allowing the model to have regular spells of rest. Somehow, I knew she would not require them. Finishing the work was everything and, with the bell for the close of classes sounding, I knew I had achieved exactly what I strove for. In still-wet colors, I had a superb full-length nude, standing with her back to the viewer and with an expression part inviting and part innocent vulnerability on her exquisitely formed face as she smiled over her shoulder. It was a masterpiece — yet I knew it was not my masterpiece.

I considered it with a sigh of satisfied relief then turned towards the podium. The girl was gone but I almost expected that would be the case just as I had known in an uncanny way that she would be there, ready posed, that morning. Equally, I knew that none of my students would have caught sight of her.

The studio was emptying rapidly, the students eager for seats in the lecture theater, that evening's guest speaker being a noted portrait painter. Miss Clatter-bridge, the middle-aged student who seemed to hold me in such awe, lingered.

'You were doing it again, Mr. Jevons,' she said. I felt she was close to alarm.

'Doing what?'

'Well, grunting and muttering as you worked at your painting. It was as if you were in a kind of trance. Oh, I wasn't prying but I looked in on you again for some advice and you were hard at it so, again, I didn't disturb you.'

'The grunting and muttering is just a habit I've fallen into, Miss Clatterbridge,' I said. 'I get deeply absorbed when I work. I don't suppose you noticed my model.'

She looked a little more frightened. 'No, I — I think you were alone.' She hastily gathered her gear and was the last student to leave the studio.

Alone, I suddenly remembered a television interview with Tinsley, the remarkable art forger of some years before.

Tinsley, undoubtedly a fine artist in his own right, produced remarkable forgeries of works by the 18th Century landscape specialist James Needham. They totally fooled all the art world, so Tinsley and the crooked dealer with whom he was associated enjoyed a brief spell of ill-gained prosperity. It fell apart when questions were asked as to why so many previously unknown Needhams came on the market through one dealer. Tinsley and the dealer were imprisoned for fraud.

After his release, Tinsley was featured on a television program in which he made the astonishing claim that, when producing the forgeries, he was taken over by the spirit of James Needham. He gave a demonstration on camera, resulting in a painting faithful in every way to the work of Needham. As he worked at great speed, Tinsley's eyes appeared glazed over and he continually grunted and gasped. He was either in some kind of abnormal state or he was an accomplished actor.

Recalling it set off a mosaic of recent memories: the haziness in which I worked; the street noises from another time; the realization that I had produced a masterpiece manifestly not my masterpiece and Miss Clatterbridge's harping on my muttering and grunting.

I returned to my cubbyhole, looked again at the finished painting which was a masterpiece, but certainly not mine. I needed no telling as to whose was that distinctive style of brushwork and that vibrant sweep of outline. This was the painting of Fred Costigan's lost love had he completed it instead of defacing it in an angry fury

The whole school was eerily empty as I carefully carried the not-yet-dry canvas through silent corridors lit by shafts of late afternoon summer sunshine. Everyone, it seemed, had gravitated to the lecture theater.

Suddenly, just as I reached the point where the Life corridor made its sharply angled turn, I was face-to-face with the girl. She was wearing her blue robe and looking at me levelly with that enigmatic smile and now I realized how, throughout the whole of my working from her pose, we had held almost no conversation. Now, free of the haziness that surrounded me during two days of painting, I wanted answers to questions from this young woman who seemed to have been seen only by myself.

Breathlessly, I asked: 'Who are you?'

The smile became yet more enigmatic and she responded in a gentle near-whisper: 'Oh, come now, you really don't need to ask, do you?'

Then, as if to confirm what I already

knew, she turned and slipped the robe from her left shoulder. Throughout the whole of her posing on the podium, she held that shoulder slightly twisted back and away from me so that I never saw the forward part of it. Now, I saw that it bore the outline of a tattooed heart that enclosed the name: 'Fred'.

'Thank you so much for what you have done,' she murmured just before she stepped back and slipped quickly around the corner.

I followed, protesting: 'Wait! Listen! I want to ask you . . . ' But she was gone, as totally as she had disappeared when I first encountered her on this same corridor a couple of days before.

Attempting to regain some composure, I carried the canvas through the quiet building and across the forecourt to my car. While carefully manoeuvring it into the vehicle to lay it on the back seat, I saw a line of writing penciled on the lower part of the canvas stretcher. It looked freshly rendered but it was not in my hand. It read: *F. Costigan, Readly's School of Fine Art, London WC1.*

February 1914. I stared at it long and hard on that summer afternoon in a month that was certainly not February and certainly not in 1914 and recognized the hand as that in which the yellowed diary from the trenches was written.

With the painting safe at home, I spotted something else for the first time: Costigan's familiar signature in a bottom corner. But I had no recollection of so signing the work just as I had no really detailed memory of producing any of it.

So there it is, secreted in my flat, a stunning work, the masterpiece of a man long dead before it was painted; the achievement of his burning desire to capture the beauty of his lost love and put it before the world. But what can I do with it? I cannot show it in a gallery as my work nor can I declare that I have discovered a lost painting by Costigan. The freshness of the paint and any scientific examination would give the lie to such a story.

I suppose I can only keep it safe with a written record of how it came to be created, ensuring that everything will eventually come to light through my will with the hope that my account of the painting's provenance will be believed.

Every time I look at it, I seem to hear, faintly but distinctly, the words of a silly popular song from a near-forgotten era:

> '*I'll make you my own*
> *In our own little home.*
> *My mad time, gladtime,*
> *Ragtime girl . . .* '

It is sung in unison by two voices, one male and one female.

And they sound blissfully happy.

3

Song of The Sea

I thought *seal,* then *woman* the instant I caught sight of the sleek and gleaming form sprawled on the verge of the road.

It was visible only briefly as we passed with our headlights piercing the night and the slashing rain. Then there was blackness again save for the twin shafts of light filled with a hail of wet bullets driving in from the sea. The windscreen wipers creaked and sighed and my wife, Leonora, leaned across from the passenger seat, trying to peer beyond them.

'Dan, there's a woman lying beside the road!' she gasped. 'I saw her there for sure. At least, I think it was a woman, someone in black. Maybe it wasn't a woman — could have been a seal.'

I bit my lip, thinking again: *woman, seal — seal woman.* An old story from my

County Mayo ancestry had come swimming up in my mind almost as soon as I saw the slumped form. I did not want to think about it but I did a u-turn, which was not easy on the narrow coast road and in stormy darkness.

'Must be someone needing help,' murmured Leonora with her hazel Indian eyes almost pressed against the windscreen. 'I had the idea she was in a black dress. Maybe she's a nun. You're never far from a convent in the west of Ireland, but there was a sort of wet gleam, like it was a stranded seal. Maybe the poor thing was hit by a car.'

Seal woman, I thought again. *Dammit, why does that notion keep coming back?*

'There!' exclaimed Leonora. 'It *is* a woman!'

I halted the car so that the lights shone on the still form on the verge of wild grass which sloped up to a gray rock wall beyond which lay the vast Atlantic, unseen in the turbulent blackness. From the ocean gusted the wind-driven rain, direct from America, as local usage had it. We left the car and, hunched against the storm, traversed the puddled coast road. All the time, foreboding was mounting in me.

She was lying face down and, soaked by the rain, the seal-like appearance was imparted by a dress, which was a close-clinging sheath. *Oh, God, why must I keep thinking of her as a seal?* harped the voice of foreboding.

Leonora reached her a fraction before myself, knelt and gently turned the woman over.

'She's alive — breathing but unconscious,' she reported.

'Any sign of an injury? Any blood or an open wound?'

'Can't see anything. We can't leave her lying here. Hell, Dan, she's only a girl — and beautiful.'

In the beam of the headlights, I saw an ivory white face. Her beauty was stunning and her eyes were closed as if in peaceful sleep. Her face was framed by long black hair that glistened richly and there was an antique quality to the way it was parted in the center. It fell in two tresses over shapely breasts that were enhanced by her tight dress of curiously modest style in spite of the way it clung. It was jet black and totally plain, with a high neck that was fastened at the throat. The sleeves were long. The skirt, too, was long and finished at the ankles, the whole garment being little more than the sort of shift worn by women in many ages and many places. It looked as if it might be made of sealskin.

Damn and blast! Why did I keep thinking of seals?

'Get her into the car and we'll take her home,' said Leonora. 'Let's hope there are no bones broken but we'll have to get a doctor to her if need be.'

'Maybe she's just some drunken tinker woman,' I growled and, at once, I became acutely aware that I was showing appalling received prejudice against the traveling people of Ireland. I knew she was something other than that but I was hedging because I was scared. That ancient story persisted in shoving itself to the front of my mind and there was a spell in the girl's beautiful face that was working in me.

Then, for an instant, Leonora turned her face away and hid her eyes as she brushed away strands of her own black hair that had straggled wetly into them. At that moment, the girl's eyes opened and she looked directly at me. Her eyes were huge and black — and yet not wholly black for they also seemed to contain a sea-green of unfathomable depth, deeper by far than any ocean of this world.

Then came the smile. It must have been fleeting but it caused me to become detached from time and space; to hang in eternity, enraptured by it.

And I heard the song for the first time. It combined with the girl's smile to draw my very soul, out of present reality to some other plane of existence. It was sung by voices that were not human, and its cadences and phrases were not assembled by any human composer. It was ancient, far more ancient than even this tradition-soaked edge of Ireland and I knew it belonged to the secret realms of the sea and it was enticing me away into those realms.

Abruptly, the experience ended and the girl's more-than-angelic face was in repose again, with the eyes closed.

Leonora was all American bustle and efficiency and she had obviously seen and heard nothing that I saw and believed I had heard.

'For God's sake, Dan, take her feet and I'll take her head. Hurry up, she could catch her death in this weather. Sometimes, you can be so all-fired indecisive.' As always when she was annoyed, she lost her slow Oklahoma drawl.

In taking the girl's feet, I saw her shoes for the first time. There were black stockings, again of that indeterminate sealskin-like material but it was her shoes that particularly took my attention as we carried her through the headlight beams. They were leather and of archaic pattern. I had seen such shoes before, in England, among the cultural treasures found in the *Mary Rose*, the long-sunken Tudor warship recovered from the deep. I knew that shoes of that kind were common throughout Europe from at least the early Middle Ages.

We placed her more or less lying on the rear seat of the car and Leonora perched on the edge of it, holding her hand. In the dim gleam from the roof-light, I saw the haunting face, once more apparently asleep.

'There's a pulse which I think is normal,' reported Leonora. 'We'd better make her comfortable until the storm blows over then perhaps we should contact the Guards. If she's been in a road accident, they'll need to know.'

I put the car into a cautious three-point turn and we set off homeward on the black, drenched road snaking along the edge of the ocean.

Leonora said: 'Too bad we don't have a phone yet but, at least, we have a guest-room of a kind since Dave's visit.'

Her younger brother, Dave, had graduated from Oklahoma State University a few months before, soon after we came to rest in Mayo and he dropped in for a couple of weeks in the course of a tramp around Europe. The cottage we bought at rock-bottom price was of unguessable age and it was perched close to the brink of a headland jutting into the Atlantic. It had no sophistications but its tiny back room made an acceptable enough guest-room provided the guest did not expect the standards of a luxury hotel. In our modest little home, I set about concluding my study of the impact of modernity on traditional Irish kinship ties and put my Ph D to use, writing on anthropological and sociological themes.

The cottage was thatched and had the feel of the 'real' Ireland I had known as a youngster when my father brought me on holidays from England to his home place nearby. With breathtaking rapidity, homes such as ours, which had sheltered generations of the same family, became forlorn shells. Beside them rose dwellings of social-climbing brashness in which lived the newer generations.

Once, the sleeping west of Ireland was synonymous with the static state but change came upon it with the power of an earthquake. Yet, there were things deep-rooted and ancient beyond time that did not change and I felt them, sensed them and *knew* them instinctively. Thus, I knew what the creature found beside the road really was from my first glimpsing of her which sent the equation *woman-seal, seal-woman* juggling through my brain.

We reached our cottage, only just visible through the sheeting rain. Such of it as could be seen had, for me, taken on an unreal appearance, just as there had been an edge of unreality to everything since we found the waif of the storm — everything, that is, save the beckoning sea song and the lure of those ocean-deep eyes.

The headlights touched the gray stone wall surrounding our small garden and even the wall, with the new rocks only recently put in by little Sean-een Durcan, seemed no longer to have the harsh solidity of Mayo rock. I thought of talkative Sean-een as we approached the house.

Leonora and I, searching for someone to repair the numerous gaps in the wall, found him in his little mason's yard in Westport. He was intrigued to learn that we were to settle on the coast and that my grandfather had been a sergeant of Civic

Guards in the region for he knew him when he was a boy.

'A grand man,' he said. 'I remember him well and why wouldn't I? He often called into our house for a sup of tea and a smoke. He was a great one for telling yarns. Him being a Galwayman and a son of a fisherman, he had many a tale of the sea and many a tale to make you shudder, too. He told me his father heard the Banshee herself, roaring something terrifying. And on the night before a death in the family, too. Arrah, he told me your family was followed by all manner of things and, begod, he wasn't joking in the way he told it, either.'

I had chuckled at Sean-een's earnest narrative, recounted with the correct degree of west of Ireland awe. When Sean-een came out to the cottage to repair the wall, Leonora was tickled pink with him. She would take him sandwiches and tea when he took a break and the pair of them would sit under the low wall beyond which was the lip of the headland and the heaving green-blue of the Atlantic. Yarns of old Ireland galore flowed out of the little stonemason to the delight of my American wife.

He told her of Grace O'Malley, the pirate queen of this coast, with her galleons and her lusty sons and how she refused to bow her knee to England's first Elizabeth whose court she visited in all her barbaric splendor. He told of fishermen's superstitions; of women of blinding beauty and heroes as tall as mountains; of ghostly beings of the mists and of saints and the cunning Little People whose line probably stretched back to the Druidic gods whom Patrick banished. Sean-een's tales were told with vigor and liberal scatterings of the Irish language. Leonora relished all of it and she appreciated how the little stonemason's narrative gifts made him kin to the tale-tellers of her own ancestry.

But she had enjoyed these yarns in the sun-blessed and salt-tanged balminess of summer, now replaced by driving rain and, in the dark, turbulent storm that now gripped the land. I knew — simply *knew* — we faced something out of the deeps and shadows of Sean-een's legends.

I parked on the grass verge beside the garden wall and we carried the girl into the cottage. We laid her out on the bed in the spare room and, in the garish electric light, we both noticed something odd about her plain and rudimentary dress.

'It's like no material I've ever seen,' murmured Leonora. 'It doesn't seem to be cloth. It's almost a kind of fur. It's so functional, so strangely old-fashioned, just a dress with no trimmings, like something that grew on her. And I can't detect any sign of undies, no ridge of a bra-strap such as a dress so tight should reveal. Dan, it's all so weird.'

She bent closer to the sleeping girl and gasped: 'And, look, she seems to be drying naturally. I thought we'd have to use a towel on her but her dress, hair, skin — everything — is almost dry while we're still wet.'

Leonora touched the dress and, as she did so, the eyes of the sleeping girl opened abruptly. Fully alert and lit, by a smoldering, malignant light, they stared directly at my wife. They showed total hatred of her. Leonora stepped back quickly. Her body stiffened and her face underwent an instant change.

Often, I had quietly noted how, in certain lights and shadows, she could look astonishingly Indian. Now, she appeared more Cherokee than I had ever seen her. Her nostrils flared and her mouth drew back in a tight, humorless grin that showed her white teeth. It was as if she sensed something about the girl on the bed through some faculty closer to an earth-origin than any I possessed. Whatever passed between the girl of the storm and my wife was some unspoken animal communication.

Then her eyes turned on me, and the flame in them died. I saw depths of water worlds in them and I heard again the sea song, enticing, drawing my soul out of me as the ancient chorus mounted.

I began to hear a voice, not through my ears but, in some way, within my head; a sentence or two in a language vaguely Irish, some form of Irish which was already ancient when the earliest monks of Hibernia lettered their first books for the glory of the God brought by Patrick.

Then it became plain English, an enticing statement raised over the seductive chant of the sea song:

'I will have you, man of the O'Hynes. We, the seal-people will have you. I will have you from the land woman . . . '

Like a man half drunk, I watched a smile spread over the face of the woman on the bed, an alluring snare of a smile. The eyes showed yet deeper ocean depths and they drew me like magnets as the chanting of the sea song rose higher.

Then the anthem rapidly faded as the eyes closed again and the face became composed in a sleep that appeared as innocent as a baby's.

Helpless as to what we should do with the girl, Leonora and I stood watching her and I tried to gather my senses once more. My wife seemed not to have noticed how I had been affected by the enticement of the eyes and the sea song. We saw the dampness of the strange dress, the pale skin and jet hair dry before our eyes; even the bedding on which she lay seemed to be dry. Once, her eyes opened and, as if attempting a hospitable truce, Leonora asked: 'Is there anything we can get you? Food? Drink?'

The girl shook her head in an emphatic negative and closed her eyes again.

'Maybe we should just leave her. She seems to be all right,' said Leonora. She clenched her fists in her defiant way and added firmly: 'But, tomorrow, Dan, we'll do something about her. Tomorrow, we get that woman — that *creature* — out of here.'

In our bedroom at the rear of the house, we turned in. Settling into the sheets, Leonora said again: 'Remember, Dan, tomorrow, we get her out of here!'

She fell asleep almost at once, perhaps not surprisingly because she'd had a busy day, topped off by the anxious business of finding the strange girl on the homeward road.

Girl? No, she was not a girl. Of that I was absolutely certain. I slipped my arm around Leonora and held her tightly, knowing that our precious oneness was being undermined. For I knew that it was by design that the creature of the storm had entered our lives and our finding her was not so much a chance discovery as a taking of bait.

I was of the O'Hynes clan that had been rooted in this Atlantic fringe of Ireland for generations and ancestral legends warned me about the true nature of the creature found beside the road. I wanted to flee with Leonora at once, but I was already more than half captured and my will was being drained. In near panic, I held my wife yet tighter, fearing that at any minute, the creature of the storm would intrude upon us, paralyzing me with the compelling allure of her sea-deep eyes.

Something of my tumbling confusion must have penetrated Leonora's slumber, for she stirred and murmured something throaty which sounded like Cherokee but, with my small knowledge of the language, I could not distinguish it.

Dear, lovable Leonora, I thought, the capable American girl under whose skin there ran a paradoxical current of Indian mysticism. Her family's Cherokee descent is a common enough one in Oklahoma and their claim of aristocratic standing among the grouping known as The Five Civilized Tribes was a valid one.

The Southern Cherokee were among the first Indians to be herded along the hundreds of bitter miles called 'The Trail of Tears', forced from their Florida home to the new Indian Territory that would become Oklahoma. The policy of displacement was devised by the old Indian-killer Andrew Jackson called Sharp Knife by the Indians. That name became a curse.

Leonora's family had deeply held traditions. One concerned an ancestor, a shaman, a medicine man of potent powers and a virtual saint among the Cherokee. He died in the harsh exile of the alien plains country soon after the uprooting. Often, I fancied I saw proud Cherokee strength in the structure of my wife's face and the melancholy race-memory of the Trail of Tears in her striking, dark eyes and they spoke of the old shaman in the family line.

All night, I lay sleepless and apprehensive while troubled thoughts roiled in my mind. I thought of Leonora's background and of my own family, which, as little Sean-een had put it, was *followed* by ancient things. And, strangely, I thought of my grandfather whom I had never known and of his place of origin, the Galway fishing village of Roundstone, called in Irish Cloc-an-Ron, which means Rock of the Seal.

Seals, seals, why was it always seals?

Again and again through that tortured night I believed I heard the chanting of the sea song, far away and almost one with the murmur of the ocean at the end of our small garden. Possibly, Leonora heard it too, for she turned and muttered several times.

At last, I dozed for what must have been a brief time and awoke to early daylight, finding that Leonora was already up and dressed in a t-shirt and skirt. She turned to me decisively.

'Dan, I meant what I said last night,' she declared. 'I want that woman — that thing — out of here. I just looked in on her and she's still sleeping . . . '

Not sleeping, I thought. Waiting her time, scheming . . .

' . . . but I want her out, pronto, Dan,' Leonora was saying. She dropped her voice and added quietly: 'I dreamed last night. Indian dreams. Understand? I dreamed of the Ponca Deer Woman!'

Befuddled, I muttered: 'Dreams? Deer Woman?' Then I thought in a disjointed way how dreams bring mystic messages to Indians, indicating paths to be taken or avoided or opening up some personal revelation of significance.

I began to dress hastily and, as I did so, I began to hear the sea song, distant at first then mounting in volume. There was a climbing tension in the air which began to take a grip on me and I was impelled to move out of the bedroom, across the kitchen and into the spare bedroom as if driven under hypnosis. I was only vaguely aware that Leonora was following me. All the time, the sea song was increasing in intensity.

I entered the spare bedroom as if ensnared, netted by an outflow of psychic energy and dragged into sea-green depths like a captured fish.

Held in thrall, I seemed to plunge into

a water world. Salty greenness crashed around me in huge, surging waves but, above it all, I heard that captivating song, chanting its age-old Irish. I was pulled deeper and deeper then, above the thunder of the waves and paeans of the sea song, I was aware of the seductive voice of the sea creature whispering in my head: ' . . . *man of the O'Hynes, I have come for you . . . I have come to take you from the land woman . . . I have come for you . . .* '

I was abruptly aware that Leonora had grabbed me from behind. With remarkable strength, she dragged me from the room and through the kitchen to the outer door. She somehow managed to open the door and push me out into the garden. I felt the grip of the psychic sea-depths lessen as I gulped fresh air and became aware of the sun in a flawless sky and the ocean, swinging in post-storm tranquility under the lip of the headland just beyond the garden wall. Leonora rammed me against the wall of the cottage and held me there. Inside my head, the sea song faded.

'We'll get the Guards, Dan,' she gasped. 'Tell them we found her and she's sick or something. There's something — something *dangerous* — about her. We need help to get her away from here. Dammit, Dan, don't look so bewildered. Our only hope is the telephone booth down at the crossroads. Get in the car, go down there and call the Guards.'

I gulped again, befuddled, fighting for breath, still partially hypnotized by the sea song and the psychic storm into which I had been plunged. Leonora lost her temper and began to hector me.

'Damn and blast you, Dan O'Hynes! What's wrong with you? I told you we must do something. I had Indian dreams. Remember? That girl is bad medicine. Dammit, I'll do it myself!'

She hastened to the car, parked outside the garden gate. I heard the engine cough into life. Almost at once, the sea chant and the illusion of my being dragged beneath the ocean began again. Alone in the garden now, I turned to face the cottage door.

The woman of the storm was emerging from it, tall and stately as a queen. She advanced on me with her arms spread wide like a woman enticing a toddler to walk towards her. The sea song mounted, the girl's ivory face was illuminated by a magically enchanting smile and the silky female voice sounded in my head: ' . . . *now I have you, man of the O'Hynes . . . we, the seal people, have you . . . follow, into my arms . . . into our kingdom . . .* '

Somehow, she had swung in front of me and was walking backward, towards the stone wall beyond which lay the drop to the sea and I was following. Sharp pearls of teeth showed in her smile and I followed, unable to help myself, yearning for her and the kiss of her mouth, led on by her and the persistent sea song. I never knew how we crossed the wall but, somehow, we were beyond it and moving towards the very edge of the headland, step by step. In a matter of seconds, I would be with her, beneath the waves and caught in some unimaginable rapture. It was a fate I was longing for with every shred of my being.

'*No!*' Leonora's scream pierced the illusion that gripped me, drowning out even the sea song and I was vaguely aware of my wife, advancing on us with her face changing.

The woman of the storm halted and turned to face her. Again, that blaze of hatred flared in her eyes and the smile was transformed into a wicked, sharp-toothed snarl.

Leonora advanced on her in a deliberate, flat-footed Indian stalking style and a metamorphosis had occurred in her face. It had become more profoundly Indian. The high cheekbones had risen yet higher and the skin had thinned, seeming to have aged, becoming parchment-like, stretched over the bone structure. Her nose had taken on a more masculine prominence and her face resembled that of an old and wise Indian.

Leonora continued towards the sea woman then, suddenly, she sent forth a guttural rising and falling of sound from deep in her throat. It was something old and yet from the New World — a Cherokee tribal chant.

The sea woman stood on the verge of the headland, rigid, staring at Leonora who was now not truly Leonora. Then, like an uncoiling spring, my wife leaped. Her hands were clawed, reaching for the sea woman's face and her chanting turned to a cross between a blood-curdling screech and a rapid-fire rattling. It was the Cherokee turkey-gobble, the ultimate challenge to an enemy. After uttering it, a warrior would either kill his adversary or die in the attempt.

As Leonora almost came to grips with her, the sea creature stretched back her mouth into a snarl and uttered the only sound we ever heard from her. Sharp and angry but mewling and pathetic at the same time. It was the bark of a seal.

She turned to me just as she twisted away from Leonora's scratching nails, giving me a last sea-green stare which held a magnetism which still haunts me yet. Paradoxically, it also contained an unmistakable menace. She sprang away from Leonora and, even above the still-sounding turkey-gobble, I heard a parting threat:

'*I will still have you, man of the O'Hynes . . . we, the seal people, will still have you . . .* '

Then she dived from the lip of the headland. She hung against the sky for an instant and, as she smote the water, I had a last glimpse of her outfit that was surely the seal-folks' collective idea of a woman's garb, stored in their consciousness from the sight of an unknowable number of drowned women over an unknowable number of centuries.

The waves closed over her and Leonora ceased her gobbling.

At length, well out to sea, a head surfaced — the unmistakable blue-gray head of a female seal. It turned and looked back at us in the way of seals when they know humans are watching. Even at that distance, I felt the intensity of its stare. Then the head disappeared.

Leonora circled her arms around my neck and put her mouth close to my ear. Now, she was in every way the old

Leonora; the transformation that made her an Indian male had passed.

'It's over, Dan,' she breathed. 'Thank God it's over.'

I could only mumble: 'You did it. You drove her away — but — but — '

'Not me alone. In a way, I was possessed. Don't try to figure it out but remember what Sean-een said about your family being followed by old things? Well, it's kind of the same with mine. Let it go at that.'

I thought of her shaman forebear and a sentence from a textbook on anthropology came to mind:

'A characteristic of the shaman is a belief in possession by some human, animal or mythic creature to the extent that the shaman *becomes* that being in reality . . . ' Then, on its heels came thoughts of the 'shape-changers' of Celtic mythology and of the Irish hero of heroes Fionn Mac Cool, who became a deer and an ear of corn among other things.

'You *became* the old shaman,' I gasped. 'But you'd driven off to the crossroad telephone. How did you turn up here just at that moment?'

'I've told you — I was possessed.'

'The old shaman,' I mused. 'I almost begin to see it: the ancient wiles of a land people against the people of the sea . . . '

'I was on the road when I had a strong intimation that you were in trouble,' said Leonora. 'Then I seemed to see big Oklahoma spaces, hear chants and smell wood-smoke. I think I came close to seeing Manitou himself, herself or whatever Manitou is. I turned and drove right back without really knowing what I was doing. And you, Dan, you knew all along what she was. Somehow, I know that you understood that she was a seal woman and that she would have you for a husband, finally taking you beneath the sea forever. I remember what Sean-een told me about seal-wives.'

'I had a shrewd idea as to what she was the moment we found her,' I said. 'But she took hold me from the start, at first in a subtle way, and I could not break free.'

'I knew she was bad medicine,' she said, stroking my head possessively. 'I felt the animal in her and knew that she was hostile to me and we'd have to fight it out sooner or later.'

'I suppose Sean-een told you the whole story,' I said.

'Yes, one day when he was fixing the wall. It was familiar, so close to the story of the Ponca Deer Woman, of whom I dreamed last night.'

I knew what she meant. In their regular ceremonial dance, the Ponca Indian girls go hand-in-hand in a ring round a fire. From nowhere, a supernatural intruder slips into the ring, a beautiful girl in a white buckskin dress. She has black, hypnotic eyes, so beautiful that the others in the ring cannot tear their gaze from them, so they never notice her feet. But those outside the ring can see that they are the hooves of a deer.

The men join the dance and choose partners. Deer Woman takes a man who is enchanted by her eyes, holds him in a tight embrace. He lies with her only one night and dies shortly afterwards. It is as well, say the Poncas for, after that one night, he is no longer a man.

The Poncas still dance in Oklahoma

and they say Deer Woman still intrudes. The young men watch for her and vow they will capture her one day. They have yet to succeed.

'Deer Woman, Seal Woman . . . it's all so familiar, Dan,' said Leonora. 'Sean-een told me how a beautiful woman one day appears, seemingly out of the sea. She is voiceless because seals do not have the gift of speech. She finds a man and he becomes obsessed with her. They live as man and wife, becoming reclusive, wholly absorbed in their love. The man becomes just as voiceless as his seal-wife. One day, she hears the call of the sea and the beckoning of the seal people. She cannot resist it, abandons her husband and runs into the waves. Her husband watches helplessly as she sinks. When her head appears it is not that of a woman but that of a seal.'

She paused, tightened her arms around my neck and whispered with an edge of fear to her voice: 'I don't like the next bit, Dan. I don't like it a bit. The abandoned husband becomes more reclusive and lives as a hermit, pining for his lost seal-wife. Then, one day, he hears the call of the ocean, runs across the shore and into the waves. Watchers on the shore see him sink. Then two heads come up from the waves — those of a pair of seals who swim away together.' She gave a shudder. 'That's why we've got to get away from here. We must go — now!'

We left immediately, although I went through it all in a half-dazed state and Leonora handled things with her usual efficiency, declaring we could arrange to sell the cottage from a distance. We spent a few nights in a Westport guesthouse and Leonora contacted her aunt in Tulsa who had recently vacated her old home for a smaller one, intending to put the old one on the market. It was still available so we lost no time in making for Oklahoma.

I was entitled to a green card for employment having worked in the United States in the recent past while Leonora entered without trouble being American born. Some casting around the academic circles of Tulsa and the university town of Stillwater brought me a schedule of part-time lecturing while Leonora took a job with a welfare agency.

Far from the sight and sound of the ocean, we were now in the midst of vast plains country where many a native has never seen the sea or smelt a salty breeze. We could think ourselves free of any threat held by a distant ocean. Yet still it came. Dimly at first, as if breaking through all the barriers of the New World, then growing in strength — that menacing and hypnotic eons old chant from the deeps, the sea song.

I tried to dismiss it as mere imagination at first but it persists, over-riding city traffic noises and carried on the night wind, whispering in from the surrounding plains. In recent weeks, it has increased its intensity and, once more, I hear that fearsome, ghostly enticement:

‘ . . . *man of the O’Hynes, I will have you from the land woman . . .* ’

I have vowed never to return to Ireland and, though I have never mentioned my haunting to Leonora, I know she senses it. Often, when the sea song comes upon me, I see her body stiffen, her nostrils flare and the shadow of subtle change crosses her face, bringing a memory of the old shaman. It is then that Leonora's Cherokee heritage seems to be my only safeguard from the menace carried by my own Celtic heritage. *But for how much longer*?

Although I am determined to keep well away from the western seaboard of Ireland, just the other day, I saw an attractive magazine advertisement, showing a thatched cottage and an ocean strand, such as I knew at Carrowmore and Bunowen in Mayo.

Its message read: '

> *No matter where you are in the United States, Ireland's international airport at Knock puts a magnificent land of magic and myth on your very doorstep*!'
>
> *On the very doorstep*!

And the sea song continues, becoming louder, enticing, beckoning, beginning to sap my will, beginning to be irresistible . . . beginning to overpower me . . .

4

The Bad Spot

Heffernan, the former journalist and a noted old soak, was holding forth in the snug of Deasy's pub. It was more or less a nightly performance with Heffernan. Well lubricated with stout, he would loudly relive the great moments of what he claimed was a sparkling career in the world of ink and newsprint during which he had encountered everyone under the sun who had any claim to fame.

Tonight, he was on about the time he interviewed Jack Doyle. The regulars, who knew him of old, were only half listening while Heffernan hooted a monologue embellished with wild swinging of the arms.

' . . . so Jack Doyle he says to me, he says: 'I'll show you how to keep up a perfect guard and hold off your opponent's attack' and he sticks up the two fists of him to shield his chin and, says he to me: 'Now, make to hit at me face and don't be afraid to use force' . . . '

Young Sullivan, an off-duty Civic Guard, was enjoying a quiet pint in a corner, mildly amused by Heffernan's antics, carried on from his regular spot in front of the bar.

' . . . so, I prepares to land him one, bunching me fist . . . ' continued Heffernan.

The stocky figure of O'Cathal in a neat civilian suit entered the snug, nodded to Sullivan and walked over to his table. O'Cathal, also off duty, was Sullivan's sergeant at the station in this outlying Dublin suburb to which Sullivan had only lately been posted.

'What is it with your man, tonight, Tom?' he inquired. 'Another lurid yarn, I suppose.'

'It's about the time he interviewed Jack Doyle — whoever he was,' said the young policeman.

'Sure, do you young fellows know nothing?' gasped O'Cathal. 'Jack Doyle was Ireland's hope in the ring. He was the boxer who did a bit of singing — or the singer who did a bit of boxing. I don't know if anyone ever worked out which.'

' . . . lunging at him with all me might,' droned Heffernan, matching the words with a windmill-like sweep of the arm and just missing the pint of a little chap standing close by. 'And I connected. For all his boxing genius, Jack Doyle couldn't guard against the clout I put on him. I totally outsmarted his famous guard and I floored him. It was all fair and square and he was on the floor, all but senseless. Now, what I've wanted to know all these years is, could I rightly claim his title?'

'What title?' piped up old Ted Kelly, another of Deasy's regulars. 'I don't remember Jack Doyle ever holding a title.'

'What?' exploded Heffernan. 'Isn't that typical of you, Kelly? An old ignoramus who doesn't even know the history of the heroes of his own country!' He turned to face Deasy's barman. 'Give me a half-one of Power's, Dennis,' he ordered. 'I need a fortifier after hearing treachery the like of that. And don't serve me from the blasted optics. I'll have it from the bottle. Put the bottle on the counter — and don't cork it up.'

'Now he's really cruising,' commented the sergeant. 'When he take shots of whiskey with his porter, he's out to give the drink a fair battering. He likes to have the bottle at hand and 'Don't cork it up' is his usual cry.'

'He'll be footless in no time if he drinks at that rate,' Sullivan said.

'Oh, he has an old-time newspaperman's capacity for it,' said O'Cathal. 'He can take on a middling heavy cargo but you'll never be able to touch him for being either disorderly or incapable He'll find his own way home as dignified and proper as an archbishop. Sure, I have some sympathy for him. It's loneliness that drives him into the pub. Never been married and has no relatives so far as I know and he's all alone in a little flat. He makes an old fool of himself but he had a considerable reputation at one time. Beyond in Fleet Street in London it was and here in Dublin before that,'

O'Cathal strode over to the bar to order for himself and the younger man as

Heffernan began another anecdote.

'Listen, did I ever tell you how I hobnobbed with an ex-king — him that became a boy king in the thirties after his old fellow was assassinated? In the old days in Fleet Street it was, when he'd been kicked out of his country by the Communists. He used to get away from all the flunkeys and ex-generals that were in exile with him by slipping away on the quiet into a little pub I knew. Nicest young fellow you could ever meet . . .'

'Are you going to tell us now, Heffernan, that you somehow took his title from him and that, by rights you're a king as well as a boxing champion?' put in old Kelly.

'Stop interrupting, you ignorant old *bostoon*, answered Heffernan. 'Dennis, fill up the pint pot and give me another half-one from the bottle — and don't cork it up. That's the old motto — don't cork it up! As I was saying, I used to go into this pub and . . . '

Closing time was past when Heffernan, well oiled though he was, made his way as dignified and proper as an archbishop to his lonely flat along the road from the hostelry.

He turned on the television for the late night news and found an excited commentator gabbling out of the screen from some outside location to which a rocky foreshore and a distant sea made a background.

'While no-one can say for sure what's caused this dreadful development, it's certainly a most serious situation and the local Gardai are carrying out a thorough investigation,' he was saying. 'Superintendent Pat Callaghan is in charge of operations. Is there anything more you can tell us, Superintendent?'

The screen was filled by a heavily built figure in uniform. 'It's too early to make a statement and we're waiting for the State Pathologist to view the bodies,' he said. 'I would, however, stress that people in this part of Mayo should not panic or listen to rumors. The authorities have matters well in hand.'

'But you can confirm that bodies have been found?' urged the commentator.

'With regret, I can. Three of them.'

'And there's talk of the possibility of more and what about these mysterious things — these creatures — that some people claim to have seen?'

'Well, I don't wish to feed conjecture and alarm,' growled the senior policeman testily. 'Our investigations are by no means complete.'

'But,' prodded the commentator, 'something odd was seen in the region of the bend on the coast road at Ballyquin just where the extensive building work is going on at the site of the new apartment complex?'

Heffernan stood transfixed and wide-eyed before the screen. He struggled to find his voice then gurgled: 'Bend in the coast road at Ballyquin . . . building works . . . mysterious creatures . . . My God, they've disturbed something at the bad spot!'

He staggered towards a corner cupboard, opened it and produced a half-full bottle of Power's whiskey. He yanked off the cork and took a strong pull of the contents then, clutching the bottle, returned to the television set which now showed a middle-aged man and a youth, both with alarmed faces.

'Mr. Jimmy Finnerty and his son, Sean, were cycling on the coast road when they saw something unusual,' the commentator was saying. 'What exactly did you see, Mr. Finnerty?'

'Well, 'twas up in the trees, just where the land rises above the bend. Scooting through the trees was a sort of thing with a body like an eel, except it had legs. And it was big — bigger than a man and I'll swear the head was something like a fish's head but somehow like a man's as well,' gabbled the man. 'I always heard that bit of the road was a bad spot and laughed about it but, begod, I believe it now. I have a feeling there were more of them up there in the trees.'

'There were,' chimed in the boy. 'I looked back and I saw three or four moving in and out among the trees and some of them were more like frogs than men . . . '

'God save us all!' mouthed Heffernan. 'It's the building works that have caused it. They've dug into places that are best left alone. And deaths have occurred. I'll have to warn them about it — at least, tell the Guards what they have on their hands . . . '

He took several more gulps of the whiskey, almost draining the bottle. On top of the evening's heavy intake of drink, this replenishment knocked his legs out from under him and he dropped to the carpet in a semi-stupor. He lay there for a spell, helpless.

And memories from the days of his youth crowded in on his fuddled brain.

* * *

Tash Burke, the news editor, tugged at the moustache that inspired his nick-name, glowered at Heffernan and told him: 'I'm sending you down the country on a feature.'

'Me, Mr. Burke?' breathed Heffernan. He was in the first flush of youth, could still hardly believe that he had actually landed a reporter's job on a Dublin daily after his fumbling start on a country weekly and, so far, had plodded warily, feeling intimidated by both the news editor and the pernickety chief reporter.

'Yes, you! I'm sending you to Mayo on a special,' growled Burke. 'I want a feature on this old coot, Shannassy, who writes that crackpot weekly column on Irish legends and myths for us. It's all rubbish but the public like it. Though summer's ending, everything's still slow apart from the antics surrounding this Hitler blatherskite beyond on the Continent and I want a solid feature or two for the weekends. Shannassy's more or less a recluse, I hear, in a cottage that was once part of an old domain in a place called Ballyquin in Mayo. Go down and get an interview with him. Play up the mystery and myth nonsense and get back for Saturday.'

With some trepidation, Heffernan set off on the assignment with Burke's instructions to find a night's cheap accommodation in Mayo and always keep the expenses down ringing in his ears.

He sought out Shannassy's obscure dwelling place which was, as an old man in the tiny village of Ballyquin told him, 'the oul' gatehouse to what's left of the

Mountcarroll estate, down yonder against the ocean.' And, to add to the young reporter's trepidation, there came a dark warning: 'Don't be lingering too long in that place. 'Tis a terrible bad spot. And that oul' *omadhaun* that's living in it needs to be watched. Sure, he should be certified in my opinion.'

The location was on a sweep of rocky coastal road, curving around a shoulder of land. On the side facing the rise of wooded land there was only the magnificent, flat panorama of the Atlantic, calm as a mill pond now but capable of storms as ferocious as any in the world when the ugly mood was on it. Against a hump of land, Heffernan found a pair of once ornate gateposts carved with what must have been armorial devices but now worn almost wholly away by the scouring Atlantic gales. A wide pathway straggled from between the posts and twisted into the trees which half hid a squat, weathered brick building.

This, thought Heffernan, must be the gatehouse. He knew nothing of the Mountcarrolls but supposed they were of the old Anglo-Irish gentry, so many of whom had long departed the land. The tumbledown gatehouse was almost as worn as the gateposts and an abundance of weeds crowded against its walls. Nervously, Heffernan rapped on its scarred oaken door, which creaked slowly open after a full minute.

A pinched, lined and scrubby-bearded face peered out suspiciously. It was hardly welcoming and Heffernan recalled the old man's observation that the resident of the place should be certified.

'Mr. Shannassy?' inquired Heffernan.

'*Professor* Shannassy,' corrected the face.

'I'm sorry. I'm Heffernan, from the *News* in Dublin. I would have phoned, but you don't seem to be on the phone . . . '

'Indeed! You haven't by any chance brought a check or two have you? The *News* owes me for a couple of articles,' cut in Shannassy sharply.

'Sorry. The paper wants me to do a piece on you. It's thought that the readers will be interested in the man who writes on old myths and legends.'

Something like a beam of satisfaction spread over the lined face. 'Better come in.' He swung the door open wider and Heffernan entered the single room of the gatehouse. It was cramped, gloomy and almost awash with books and documents. From somewhere among the debris, Shannassy found a chair and shoved it towards his visitor.

It proved a difficult interview. Shannassy was reluctant to reveal too much about himself and it emerged that he had only withering scorn for the academic establishment. He had, it seemed, awarded himself the title of professor. 'I have more right to it than the stuffy old idiots up at Trinity or University College in Dublin,' he growled. 'All they ever did was learn a few oddments from a clutch of textbooks. I've spent years and years delving into the byways and backroads of ancient Irish culture. I've made it my business to discover things at ground level among the people of the land who're still steeped in the old stories and traditions. You have Irish, I suppose?'

'Of course,' said Heffernan.

'Aye, the sanitized Irish shoved into you by the Christian Brothers, no doubt, but not the old time, raw Irish of long ago. You'll know the meaning of the word *piseog*?'

'Yes — an old folk-superstition.'

'And are you a countryman at all?'

'More or less. Originally from a small place in Kilkenny.'

'Then you'll know there's many a *piseog* to be found around every corner in all the Four Kingdoms of Ireland and the old folks are stuffed full of 'em. Well, I've spent my time investigating all the old superstitions, tales, legends, call them what you will and I went right to the roots of the people to find 'em. No foostering around in university libraries for me, though I've collected my share of books and manuscripts as you can see by looking around.'

Heffernan gave an inward sigh. He had not yet produced his notebook but could see there was no hope of honing his youthful interviewing skills on this old eccentric. Shannassy was a talker and seemed set fair to talk a blue streak without Heffernan ever getting a word in. Still, he thought, if he memorized something of what the old man said he would probably get the makings of a decent feature.

'And I'll tell you this: there's more truth in the old tales that have never died out than the big city people with their wirelesses and aeroplanes ever dreamed of — and some of 'em are damned uncomfortable and downright *dangerous* truths,' breathed Shannassy mysteriously. 'I suppose you know the sort of place the people call a bad spot around your own home place and probably more than one?'

'I do for sure,' said Heffernan.

'Don't be telling me — I'll tell you. The dark bit near the trees on the quiet road where a man suddenly sees the old uncle, whose funeral he was at when he was a mere child, standing in the shadows and looking at him sorrowfully then disappearing entirely. The twisty bit of an old *boreen* lane, which half the village will avoid at dusk for fear of being chased by one of the worst of fairy manifestations, a black pig. The spot from which a mother will keep her baby at all costs lest the fairies snatch the child away for ever. I know them all — and let me tell you that the old *piseog* yarns are not to be scorned. There's often a deep truth going right back to the beginning of Celtic times lying at the bottom of them, no matter how its been twisted down the centuries.'

Shannassy paused and swept a hand towards the grimy mullioned window. 'Take this location for instance. There's hardly a more desperate bad spot in all Ireland than this place — that bend in the road out yonder has been notorious since the drying of the Flood. Dark tales were told of this edge of the ocean centuries ago, some of 'em concerned with battle, murder and sudden death and some, much more chilling, from beyond the misty curtains of the Celtic past. The place has attracted tragedy persistently. Only recently, in the troubled times, the big house belonging to the Mountcarrolls who owned the domain for centuries was burned down by one side or the other.

Then, the local rebel flying column lay in ambush on the land above the bend and put paid to a convoy of Black and Tans as they came roaring down the road. A couple of years later, in the Civil War, with Irishman fighting Irishman, Mick Collins's new National Army played the same trick, surprising a squad of Republican irregulars. Some dreadful things have taken place hereabouts and it was the reputation of the place that made me settle here when I heard the old gatehouse still stood and was for sale.'

'You mean you came to live here in spite of the reputation of the place?' asked Heffernan.

'Indeed I did. Out of the pursuit of scholarship and because I was deeply interested in old Lord Maurice Mountcarroll who ruled the roost here in the early Nineteenth Century.

'He was different from the usual run of hunting and boozing Mountcarrolls; a decent landlord to his tenants and a scholar, deeply interested in the old legends and traditions of the people. He was forever searching for the relics of the old Celtic world. History more or less forgot him but I found a yarn saying he discovered something of importance here on this very land.' Shannassy leaned forward and dropped his voice to a near-conspiratorial whisper.

'Something from the old times it was — something sinister and downright dangerous. For years, just under the surface of the folk-memories of the local population, there was a belief that old Lord Maurice found this horrifying secret thing in the woods climbing up above this old ruin of a house and took great pains to conceal it from view, hoping it would never be found. It was so shocking he labored with his own hands to bury it deep instead of having any of his tenants do the job. Somehow, however, word of it got out and so this region's already established reputation as a bad spot was intensified. I can tell you the *piseog* surrounding this place is one to beat them all.'

Heffernan's pulse quickened. Now, it looked as if he was about to capture his story. Surely, the old eccentric was going to reveal something about this remote edge of the land which would give him the core of a piece which would be eye-catching on the features page.

'That was what brought me here,' continued Shannassy in his dramatic whisper. 'There was nothing concrete at first, just the old tale but I began to search as soon as I settled here and, though it took months — *I found it*!'

Heffernan reached for the pencil in the top pocket of his jacket but Shannassy held up a cautioning hand. 'Not so fast. I can't have you spreading this secret all over the world. It could cause a wild panic. At the same time, I'm the only mortal creature who knows the truth of it and I'm on the edge of the grave so I have to pass it on to someone — but, if I reveal it to you, for God's sake don't print it.'

Heffernan frowned. He was being forced into a corner. He was here to find a story and it looked as if he had succeeded but this old eccentric was laying down conditions he could not accept. Young though he was, he had absorbed the journalistic dictum that he should never allow any censorship or doctoring of his material except by his editorial superiors. However, old Shannassy pressed on, not allowing him an opportunity to object.

'Come on outside and I'll show you something that'll make your hair stand — but don't reveal a word of it, particularly to the so-called academic and archaeological crowd up in Dublin. They'd be down here like a cloud of locusts.'

As if powered by the chance of at last unburdening himself of a long held secret, Shannassy made for the door with Heffernan in his wake. Outside, the salty breeze swept up from the ocean, rustling the trees, which hemmed in the small gatehouse and clothed the rise of land above it. Heffernan shuddered and not wholly because of the breeze. Shannassy tramped up an ill-defined track through the trees with remarkable alacrity for an old man.

'Don't the trees themselves tell you this place is odd?' he asked. 'They're clue enough that things are not right here

— that it's a bad spot.'

'The trees?' queried Heffernan, bewildered.

'The very fact that they are here,' growled the old man. 'There's devil a tree to be found all along this section of the coast. How could there be with some of the worst gales in Europe sweeping it regularly for century on century, giving no tree a chance to flourish in peace? Yet, here, in this peculiar spot, we have a virtual forest, cloaking the land — as if nature herself is intent on concealing something and defying her own rules to do it. And that was the truth of it, Mr Heffernan — until old Lord Maurice Mountcarroll found what was being concealed.'

Old Shannassy led the way deeper into the trees until they came to a small clearing in the center of which there reared a hump of earth covered in wild grass. 'And here,' he said, 'is the same terrifying thing that old Mountcarroll found.'

He dropped to his knees in front of the mound and yanked away several loose sods of turf that concealed a large stone slab. Heffernan bent to look closer and saw that letters and curious symbols were carved into the stone. The handiwork was obviously ancient and, while there was a familiarity about the letters, he could make out only one or two. The language was vaguely Irish but he could not decipher any meaning.

He heard Shannassy chuckle behind him: 'It might just as well be Greek to you, eh? That's because it's not the Gaelic League kind of Irish they gave you in school. It's a damn' sight older than that. It's ancient Irish, out of a distant time, and you'll be unfamiliar with the alphabet. But, look, this symbol is an 'f' and this one an 'i', so what would you make of the whole word?'

'It looks like 'Formorii',' pronounced Heffernan.

'Exactly. And did you ever hear of the Formorii?'

'Some kind of legendary folk, I think,' ventured Heffernan. 'Didn't they go to live underground and become the Little People — the fairies?'

'You're confused but near the mark,' said Shannassy. 'It was the Tuatha De Danaan who went to dwell in glittering underground palaces to become the fairies of popular legend. They were the last race of magical gods to rule ancient Ireland. The Formorii were monstrously ill-shapen and cruel sea-creatures who battled the Tuatha De Danaan and were defeated by their superior magic. The Tuatha De Danaan, remember, were dab hands at magical underground engineering and they created a tunnel through which they banished the Formorii into the ocean. Magically, this tunnel was the only link between the world of the Formorii and that of us mortals. It was the only means by which they could be sent from the land — *and the only means by which they could return to it*.

'For there was the usual Achilles heel factor, you see. The magic formula of the Tuatha De Danaan lacked a safeguard against the sea monsters using it as a way back, though it was securely sealed. Down the ages, the place was known as the very site of the tunnel and, long after the disappearance of the Tuatha De Danaan, when a written language was in being, precautions were taken to post a warning. The seal was reinforced and marked by this stone.'

'And what does this lettering say?' asked Heffernan.

'It says —

'*Through this tunnel were driven the Formorii, the unclean things of the ocean into the waves which created them. Let it remain sealed for ever for fear of their using this, their only gateway, to emerge again and imperil the people of the land.*' '

'So is there really a tunnel behind the stone?' asked Heffernan.

'That's what old Lord Maurice believed and I believe it, too,' confirmed Shannassy. 'So far as I can decipher these other symbols, they tell of the place being sealed with ceremonies by the old druidical priests who flourished before the arrival of St. Patrick. I hope to high heaven that the tunnel remains corked up for all time. If someone shifts this slab — uncorking the tunnel, so to speak — the Formorii could swarm ashore again and perpetrate who knows what horrors. It's a secret I've kept for years and I admit I'm relieved to have shared it. I've placed a big burden on you, young fellow. Be careful what you do with it. I'm trusting you won't be the means of bringing the academic crowd and the gawping tourists down on me.'

Heffernan left Ballyquin in a dilemma. His brief was to return with a pen-portrait of the man who wrote his paper's column on Irish folklore but he had scarcely interviewed Shannassy and he was returning with quite different data. As the old man had said, he had been burdened with quite a responsibility when informed of the ancient stone and the terrible secret it guarded. Shannassy did not want the wider world to know about this outlet for the monstrous Formorii and Heffernan found he liked the eccentric old recluse and he had no desire to betray his trust. But what was he to do with the knowledge imparted to him? He was, after all, a newspaperman and he had a story of shattering importance if one shared old Shannassy's belief in the potency of the old legends. Should he give it to the world or should he hush it up and manufacture some sort of word profile of old 'Professor' Shannassy to suit the needs of the feature page?

It was not a day when the youngest of reporters on Irish papers had the luxury of chasing assignments in cars and Heffernan had reached this remote corner of County Mayo by train and an infrequent local bus. Heading back to Dublin by the same means, he cudgeled his brains as to the course he should take. Throughout the journey, he sat deep in thought and did not even while away the time with a book or newspaper. By the time his train steamed into Westland Row station, he was still at a loss as to how he should handle the material he had gathered. He had, however, reached a conclusion concerning the tunnel 'corked up' by the stone bearing its dire warning. The whole thing, of course, was a complete fraud.

Old Shannassy, with his total faith in

the ancient tales, might believe it to be authentic, but it was quite likely simply an elaborate device to keep unwanted intruders such as poachers off the Mountcarroll lands. Lord Maurice Mountcarroll was probably as fiercely intent as any other landlord of his time on keeping his domain and its game private. Shannassy might accept him as a genuine scholar of the old lore, but it was quite conceivable that he had set up the stone himself and created the legend of some sinister mystery hidden in the woodland. Knowing that the local peasantry held a generations old *piseog* about the locality and had it marked as 'a bad spot', he probably set on foot a new legend to ward off unwanted intruders.

Yes, thought Heffernan, that was doubtless the whole truth of the matter. But, as he mounted the steps of the office, he was still in a dilemma as to what he was going to write.

Tash Burke met him in the corridor. 'About time you showed up!' he roared.. 'Get into the reference library and dig up two columns of background stuff on modern Poland and I want it quick.'

'But I've just come back from seeing old Shannassy in Mayo . . . ' began Heffernan.

'Forget about that hogwash. You can spike it for all time, so far as I'm concerned,' growled Burke. 'Dammit, man haven't you seen a paper or heard the news? The country is in a sweat about whether De Valera will join the British in a full-scale war or remain neutral. Hitler has massed his troops on the Polish border and is about to invade at any minute!'

* * *

Heffernan's head cleared to some degree. He was lying on the carpet of his flat and an urgent voice was issuing from the television set: ' . . . no clear picture as to what is happening has yet emerged and we are awaiting a government statement. It has been confirmed however, that a large contingent of troops has been sent to Mayo, and all police leave has been cancelled. We understand the British government and those of other European nations are being kept constantly informed of events at Ballyquin . . . '

'Ballyquin,' muttered Heffernan, picking himself up. 'My God! Ballyquin — the bad spot!'

Tangled thoughts raced through his mind: the recollection of what the television had revealed before he passed out — something about work on building a new complex of flats — startling reports of strange creatures seen in the woods, things which might have resembled fish, frogs or men and of bodies being found — and the memory of a story he tackled long ago concerning an eccentric old recluse with outlandish theories — a story which was overwhelmed by the pressing urgencies of another day and which became forgotten then disappeared with the years of his youth.

The television set was still jabbering: ' . . . we keep receiving rumors of yet more sightings of the creatures along the west coast. There are also reports of yet more killings but we emphasize that these are only rumors and the authorities are stressing the need to keep calm . . . '

Heffernan staggered towards the door and held on to the jamb to catch his breath. Now, he began to see the pattern of events. There was a building boom in holiday homes along the west coast these days. Some company had acquired the Ballyquin land, the 'bad spot', the bend in the road overlooking the Atlantic, an ideal site for a set of luxury flats. They must have moved in with diggers to clear the woodland and . . .

'Great God!' he panted. 'I have to warn them about the tunnel . . . the Formorii . . . they'll be coming into the land in droves . . . .'

He remembered the Civic Guard station only a short distance away and hastened into the street. Immediately, the cold air hit him and induced further wooziness because of the evening's heavy intake of alcohol. He stumbled along the pavement and caught sight of a uniformed man ahead of him, walking briskly in the same direction. It looked like the new young peeler, Sullivan, whom he had seen earlier in the pub. 'Garda Sullivan!' he mouthed slurringly.

'Tell 'em to cork it up! They have to hurry and cork it up!'

The policeman turned briefly with a puzzled look and continued walking.

'D'you hear me?' persisted Heffernan. 'I have something important to tell you.'

'Behave yourself and go home,' retorted Sullivan over his shoulder. 'I haven't time to listen to you now.' He continued his quick walk with Heffernan tagging behind shouting some hardly coherent message.

Other uniformed figures were making their way into the door of the station and Sergeant O'Cathal whom Sullivan had so recently seen enjoying his evening off was now standing in the doorway, also in uniform and looking agitated.

'What's happening?' asked Sullivan. 'I got a phone call at home telling me to report for duty and quick.'

'Cork it up!' wailed the voice of Heffernan in the background. 'They have to cork it up!'

'All hell is let loose in the west,' said the sergeant. 'You and a crowd of the younger men are being flown down to Mayo at once. Matter of keeping public order and helping the army out. Everybody who can be rounded up is being sent there. I never knew the like of it.'

Again, Heffernan's warning rang on the night air: 'Cork it up! Cork it up!'

'What the hell is your man blathering about?' asked the sergeant. 'Sure, for years '*Don't cork it up!*' has been his watchword when he's in the vicinity of the whiskey bottle and now he's yelling for it to be corked up. I suppose the gargle has at last driven him around the bend entirely.'

Frowning, he watched Heffernan grab the shoulder of one of the officers who was hastening into the station and begin hooting his message. Then, frustrated, O'Cathal pushed forward and clutched Heffernan's arm.

'I've heard enough from you,' he growled. 'We're in the thick of the damnedest crisis ever known and you're obstructing officers in the exercise of their duties. I'm jugging you for the night!'

Heffernan found himself propelled into the station charge room and up to the desk of the duty sergeant. Sullivan followed on their heels.

'Put him in the guest room until he sobers up, Paddy,' O'Cathal instructed the duty sergeant. 'And he's lucky I'm not charging him.'

Heffernan's unheeded plea to '*Tell them to cork it up!*' was sounding thinly from the cell as Sullivan persisted in his questioning of O'Cathal: 'But what's going on in Mayo? Television is giving out something about mutilated corpses being found and what sound like wild animals rampaging all over the place.'

O'Cathal shoved him into a quiet corner of the charge room. 'That's not even the half of it, Tom,' he murmured with a shudder. 'There's a whisper from headquarters that — though God knows why they should target the butt-end of Mayo — we're being invaded by the Martians!'

5

Fir Gorta

'The Yank is coming back in a couple of weeks,' announced Dotie Clenahan across the bar as she drew a pint of stout for Tommy Lynch. 'Staying for quite a while, too.'

'The Yank? Mr. Criswell is it?' sniffed Lynch, reaching for the glass. 'I never liked him.'

'Oh, is that so?' hooted Mick O'Carroll who had been at odds with Lynch ever since they were youngsters in the village school fifty years before. 'Well, when he was here last year and stood a round in this very pub, I noticed you were the first to get your snout around what was on offer.'

'And why wouldn't I?' responded Lynch. 'Do you think I'd be so ill-mannered as to scorn a man's kindness and him a stranger among us? Still, ain't I entitled to say I didn't much care for him if that's the case?'

'You didn't say that at all. You said you never liked him,' countered O'Carroll. 'It didn't stop you fawning on him with your Mister Criswell this and Mister Criswell that and all the time squinting to see would he produce his wallet again, you old hypocrite.'

'All the same, you must admit he had an annoying way with him — all that loud heartiness,' said Larry Donovan, the young Civic Guard who was off duty and standing at the far end of the bar. 'There was something not quite right — something suspicious.'

'Hah! Isn't that only because you're a policeman?' scorned little Mary Crowe from her regular corner table. 'You should hang up your suspicions with your tunic. His hearty way is nothing but the American style. He deserves a bit of understanding, him being without a wife or chick or child nor anyone in the world so far as I know.'

'Well, there was something odd in the way he was always hanging around the remains of the Big House,' answered the policeman. 'Almost every day, he was in the vicinity of the house and the lands around them.'

'And, God knows, that's a place the rest of us would keep well away from, knowing the reputation of it and those who lived in it,' muttered Mick O'Carroll with the suggestion of a shudder.

'Just the American way again,' said old Mary. 'They love bits of old castles and manor houses since they say they have no real history of their own. Hatred of the D'Albert family might linger among the likes of us, but Mr. Criswell knows nothing about them and their ways.'

'And damned bad ways they were, too,' growled Tommy Lynch. 'We Irish might be fond of dwelling on past wrongs and maybe it's not a good thing — but there was reason enough for ill-feeling against the D'Albert family and bad landlords like them. Think of the Big Hunger when the potato crops were blighted and people hadn't a crust to eat or a penny for rent and the D'Alberts drove them off their lands. Even pulled the thatches off their cabins when they lay starving or sick with the cholera — '

'Don't be giving us the whole litany, Tommy,' put in Mary Crowe. 'The Famine was a long time ago and, anyway, not all of the D'Alberts were villains. They say Lady D'Albert was a good woman who did what she could for the people but her husband, old Lord Hugh, put a stop to her good works. And those were times when a woman was under her husband's thumb.'

'Well, for once, I'll agree with you, Tommy,' said O'Carroll. 'It was a good day when the last of the D'Alberts cleared off from here and into obscurity.'

Dotie Clenahan, a buxom widow who owned the pub combined with a bed-and-breakfast service that flourished in the holiday season, listened to the exchanges with her arms folded over her bosom. All the time, with pursed lips, she maintained an expression of having some secret yet to impart. And impart it she did.

'When the Yank, Mr. Criswell, wrote to me, he said he's coming with a special object in view. He's bought what's left of the Big House and the lands and he's coming intending to settle there,' she said. 'He'll drop in here for meals, but he'll be buying a big trailer so he can live up there and oversee the renovation of the place.'

There was a collective gasp then a silence, broken at length by O'Carroll. 'Bought the ruins of the Big House and the lands?' he echoed. 'Does he know anything of the horrors lingering around the place?'

'Does he know,' intoned Mary Crowe darkly, 'about the field that comes down to the roadway and the humps that are in it?'

'The field where you claim the *fir gorta* got you when you were a slip of a colleen?' said Tommy Lynch scornfully. 'Sure, there's no such thing. That's all a *piseog* — a daft country superstition.'

'It is not!' emphasized Mary indignantly. 'I was attacked by the *fir gorta* and it's lucky I was to stagger out of that field alive. I'm haunted by it yet.'

'The *fir gorta*? What's that?' queried Garda Donovan. The young policeman was a Dubliner in his first country posting. Raised in the city, he was as yet unfamiliar with much country lore.

'Arragh, don't pay any attention to it,' growled Tommy Lynch. 'It's just a damnfool *piseog*.'

'Well, I experienced it and I know what I'm talking about,' persisted Mary Crowe. 'I walked over one of those humps without meaning to — then it had me!'

At which point, Dotie Clenahan imparted yet more choice information. 'Here's something more to drop you in your tracks,' said she. 'He said in his letter that he's taken the name of D'Albert and tacked it on to his own name. It seems he's found that part of his family is descended from the D'Alberts who blew into America after leaving here. Criswell-D'Albert he's after calling himself now.'

There was a collective clunk of drinking vessels being thumped down on tables in astonishment.

'So that was it,' said the young policeman. 'He was investigating the old family seat.'

'A D'Albert, back here in Ballygrill?' gasped Tommy Lynch. 'Wasn't the whole townland rejoicing to be rid of them generations ago?'

'It was,' agreed Mary Crowe. 'God knows, I wish him no harm — but does he know about the curse?'

'Another *piseog*?' asked Larry Donovan with a wry smile.

'You may smirk all you like,' declared old Mary, 'but there was a time when everyone in this townland knew the curse and could recite it. It was put on the last of the D'Alberts as they departed. The whole breed of them were named as thieves who stole their lands in the first place and rogues in the way they governed them ever since. The curse of the famished masses who died in the Big Hunger was pronounced on any D'Albert who settled in the region of Ballygrill ever again.' She paused, shook her head and breathed: 'Begod, it's sorry I am for the Yank if he's come here bearing that name. Remember the old Irish saying that a curse settles not on sticks nor stones but on flesh and bones!'

* * *

Warren Criswell, now hyphenated into Criswell-D'Albert, felt pleased with himself as he settled into the mobile home established beside the tumbledown and ivied walls of the old Big House, which he now owned. In a few days, the architect and representatives of the building company would arrive to consider renovating the property. As yet, he had only vague plans as to the development of the lands but he intended to make something profitable out of them, thereby earning prestige in the community. Profit, after all was always the motivation of his life.

He was a large, middle-aged man whose girth and well-fed jowls spoke of an existence well cushioned by profit. As plain Warren Criswell, he had considered himself to be above the usual run of men; but deed poll had transformed him into Warren Criswell-D'Albert so he now felt himself to be an aristocrat. He had discovered that his mother had distant connections with the D'Alberts who had once owned lands in the far west of Ireland, hard by the mighty Atlantic, but he knew almost nothing of the now died-out D'Alberts. A book on old Irish families showed that, like all Norman-Irish, the D'Alberts had a coat-of-arms and could there ever be a more impressive mark of aristocracy? On slight authority, he adopted both surname and coat-of-arms.

It had long been his plan to cease his active world business interests and settle in some obscure place and when he found that, for decades, the remains of the old D'Albert mansion and a portion of their lands had been available for purchase, his path was clear. He knew little of Irish affairs and left all the practicalities to a firm of Dublin lawyers but it seemed that, when the Irish Free State came into being, the D'Albert lands went into the hands of something called the Land Commission. Portions of land were sold off to become farmsteads but the shell of the old family mansion and some surrounding land remained on the books.

Criswell paid a summer visit to the region, found the village of Ballygrill to be a pleasant little place and the people relaxed and colorful in a specifically Irish way. They seemed to take to him as he lodged comfortably at the pub where Mrs. Clenahan provided cosy accommodation far different from that of Dublin's sanitized tourist-trap hotels. In a friendly way, the locals called him 'the Yank' for it seemed that in Ireland anyone from over the Atlantic, even from reaches deep below the Mason-Dixon Line was a 'Yank'.

Canniness had always been an ingredient of his make-up so he never told anyone why he spent so much time with his camera tramping the old D'Albert holdings and photographing the ruined 'Big House'. At the end of his stay, his mind was made up: he would have the old house and the land and quit Los Angeles for this quiet retreat — which some might call his bolt-hole.

Now with his many international business interests sold off, he had arrived in his little kingdom, feeling carefully shielded from the outside world. And he had a great desire to be shielded.

For years he had played his own slippery game, unknown to his various partners. There were numerous deals done through sets of lawyers, different ones for different corporations and Warren Criswell was the only one to profit from them. Money in huge amounts was salted away in countries where the accounts were untouchable by probing officialdom and the Internal Revenue Service of the United States — and to which Criswell alone had access. Now and again, there were protests from do-gooders concerning South American mining operations and Asian and African logging projects profiting Criswell's legitimate concerns which caused landslides floods, the destruction of villages and the starvation and impoverishment of already poor populations. He and his associates always rode them out and, all the time, Criswell maintained his up-the-sleeve activities unknown to those same associates.

Here on the obscure and isolated western edge of Ireland, he hoped soon to drop the very name of Criswell and sport only his newly adopted one. It would be highly satisfactory for his old name to become forgotten by the world of international business and those who probed into it although steps would be taken to ensure that his profits continued.

For the plump, cheerful-faced new owner of the ruined Big House who brought back the name of D'Albert to Ballygrill was several kinds of devious and heartless rogue.

* * *

Even on his first morning after arriving in the luxury trailer home he had acquired in Dublin and towed across country, Criswell-D'Albert began to feel that something was wrong. He brought packed food with him which he consumed on his first night parked beside the ruin and, in the morning, went in search of one of Mrs. Clenahan's excellent breakfasts.

It was a bright spring day and he decided to walk to the village, following the ribbon of road that was easily accessible from the site of the old house. He walked energetically, rejoicing in the fresh air with its strong salt tang from the nearby ocean.

Remembering the joviality of the pub from his visit the previous year, he almost expected a cheerful 'Caed mille failte' — 'A hundred thousand welcomes' — for he had established himself as a hearty fellow. It failed to show up.

The place was empty save for Dotie Clenahan who was cordial enough but by no means gushing Was there, he wondered, something cautious, guarded, even suspicious in her attitude when she greeted: 'Well, is it back again you are? You'll be needing a decent breakfast, so.'

She served the meal but, instead of staying at the bar for one of her usual chats, she rather pointedly disappeared back into the kitchen, leaving him alone. Two farming men arrived, sat at a nearby table and were served by Dotie who then disappeared again. They responded politely but curtly to his observations on the weather and ate without further conversation, occasionally casting him glances that he felt were heavily suspicious.

He had an uncomfortable feeling that he was not welcome at the pub and certainly the usually amiable Mrs. Clenahan appeared to be intent on keeping out of his way. The cheerfulness he had encountered at the hostelry the previous year was certainly lacking.

He strolled back to his trailer in an unsettled mood and, when passing a field that was part of his lands, isolated by a gray fieldstone wall traditional to this region and adjoining the road, paused to consider the curious grassy humps it contained. He had not discovered what those humps were and had never set foot in the field. Someday soon, he told himself, he would make inquiries about the meaning of those mounds.

Back at his trailer, he made himself busy unpacking his belongings and investigating the gaunt walls and roofless skeleton of the old D'Albert mansion, making notes and sketching tentative plans for renovation to be discussed with the architect.

Remembering the cool social atmosphere of the pub, he avoided the place and made a scratch lunch at the trailer then busied himself around the mined rooms again. The balmy spring afternoon lengthened towards evening by which time, he began to feel the need of a substantial meal Perhaps, the crowd which generally gathered at the pub in the evenings would impart a more welcoming atmosphere, he thought, so he set off towards the village again.

If anything the larger number of customers intensified the sense of unwelcome. Dotie Clenahan was just as uncommunicative; the faces remembered from last year offered only curt acknowledgements and the celebrated hundred thousand welcomes of Ireland were decidedly absent. Even his offer to stand a round for a group who eagerly quaffed with turn the year before was almost rudely rebuffed. It was all too evident that no one wished to hold a conversation with him and, though he was addressed as 'Mr. Criswell' a couple of times, it was noticeable that the proudly adopted name of D'Albert was not appended. Nobody offered a 'Good night' as he left the premises into the warm evening.

Tramping back to the ruined mansion again, he felt heavy-hearted, certain now that all Ballygrill was cold-shouldering him. Furthermore, there was a heavy feeling of depression in the air that seemed to increase with every step. It was particularly oppressive at the point where the field with the intriguing humps met the road.

Criswell-D'Albert found that he could not pass the evening-shrouded field without stopping and looking over the wall at the grassy mounds. As he did so, he felt an almost physical weight of depression that caused him to give an involuntary shudder. He hastened away, with a clammy sweat all over his body.

That night, he lay in his bunk, uneasy and unable to sleep. Outside, the western Irish countryside was enfolded by darkness, deadly silent.

Until the whisperings started.

At first he was not sure they were whisperings. It sounded like the murmur of the breeze in the trees, only just audible. Then it grew slowly louder. Voices. There were definitely voices — sibilant, enticing, calling the name '*D'Albert . . . D'Albert . . . D'Albert . . .*'

He shuddered and pulled the sheets over his head. It was surely the wind — only the wind, circulating around the gaunt walls of the old ruin against which his trailer was halted.

But he knew there was no wind that tranquil, balmy spring night.

The sound strengthened, became higher and more insistent: '*D'Albert . . . D'Albert . . . D'Albert . . . outside . . . come outside . . . come outside . . . come outside . . .*'

He tried to convince himself that it could only be some freak of geography caused by the position of the ruined house on the slightly elevated land and the breeze from the nearby Atlantic circulating through the empty window-spaces in the crumbled walls of the old building. He knew, though, that the night was breezeless. But the voices persisted, still audible however deeply he tried to bury himself into his bunk with his hands clasped over his ears.

And, with the voices, the oppressive weight of inescapable and menacing depression bored yet further into his consciousness. Had everything in this once welcoming land — the people who now offered hardly a friendly word and showed him only a surly, steely resentment, as well as the very earth and air of the place — turned enemy? Outside the flimsy shell of his trailer home, there now seemed only a cauldron of hostility into which he was being enticed by the beckoning voices. For the voices were there, no matter how he tried to shut them out. They, like the tangible menace of the surrounding atmosphere, were eating deeper into his brain, repeating the name he had adopted and brought back into this land: *D'Albert! D'Albert! Come outside . . . come outside . . . D'Albert, D'Albert* . . . until he could stand it no longer.

He rose, telling himself unconvincingly that it must all be a prank. Youngsters from the village must be lurking outside, perpetrating a practical joke on 'The Yank', the sophisticated big city stranger.

He staggered, barefoot and in his pyjamas, to a window and looked out. There was only the dark night — *and the voices, louder, insisting, increasingly enticing* . . .

Then, suddenly, something appeared. Ghostly, gray, at first small and insubstantial, there was the shape of a human. It was a child, only just outside the window, looking directly at him with large, accusing eyes set in a head that seemed too big for the little body. A ragged, Asiatic child such as those shown on the posters of the impudent and annoying do-gooders who picketed and sometimes invaded the offices of his business concerns, demanding an end to their overseas mining, logging and other enterprises. It was those damned campaigners who had somehow discovered his movements and somehow pursued him here!

No, it was not a poster — it was a child, a tattered, starved, accusing child. Then another appeared at its side, then another, then a skeletal, ragged woman cradling a small baby in her arms, then another and an emaciated, stooped Asiatic man . . . all of them seemingly conjured up out of the very night air and all staring at him with huge, accusing eyes.

And there were voices. Always, the voices.

It was a trick, Criswell-D'Albert thought, trying to order his jangled nerves. The campaigners, those who alleged he and his associates created starvation in the developing world, had devised some form of projection of images, probably by electronics. He barged towards the door, flung it open and charged out into the night. They were out there — the starveling ghosts, crowding the field outside the trailer, simply standing there, facing him, dumbly accusing — always accusing.

He lurched towards the figures, waving his arms as if to shoo away a flock of geese. But he could not reach them. They were always paces away from him. And the voices chanted the name of D'Albert continually as he blundered on through the field, not even aware of the ground under his bare feet. Then, around the figures, a ghostly landscape was evolving. He saw a backdrop of forests, then the ragged stumps of trees, thousands of them, felt warm tropical air, saw a panorama of tumbled primitive homes and felt the poverty and degradation. He stumbled on into the night, hoping that, somehow, he could physically grapple with this nightmare and strangle it.

The sibilant voices enticed him and, abruptly, the panorama changed. He was now in the field that slanted away down to the road into the village, the field with the mysterious grassy mounds.

There were more figures and a new, grotesque landscape taking shape around him.

Ghostly at first, then more solidly, there appeared a sorry array of humanity: children, women and men. They were gaunt, barefoot, clad in wretched rags and all with heads reduced to mere skulls in which there again burned huge, accusing eyes. He was in the midst of them, trying to dismiss them with frantically waving arms.

'Go away!' he screeched in a cracked

and hysterical voice. 'Go away! Leave me alone!'

But they multiplied. More and more of them surrounded him, a wretched horde of famished phantoms, who were there and yet not there when he tried to strike out at them. Once more, he saw shawled, skeletal women with tiny scraps of humanity in their arms; children with stick-like limbs and bellies extended by want of nourishment; ragged old men and women whose bent and frail bodies quivered with ague. And there were ghostly buildings: the low, deep-thatched cabins of the peasant Irish of long ago but bereft of any cosy, rural charm. Some of them were tumbled and the thatches of others had been forcibly dragged off while others had burning thatches that sent up a reek of smoke to fog the horrifying tableau surrounding Criswell-D'Albert.

Then his bare foot struck one of the mounds in the ground and he stumbled to sprawl full length over the grassy hump. Immediately, the agony hit him — a pain in the pit of his stomach like no pain he had ever known. It was a wrenching, agonizing knife, slicing into his innards. He gave a strangled, gasping cry and tried to rise but fell forward, writhing as the pain hit again, this time even more burningly intense. He sprawled on the small hump in the land and rolled in growing agony, with his legs drawn up to his chest. He was dimly aware that the starving phantoms were crowding around him, watching him with haunted eyes that bore no pity. They were all there: a horde of living near-corpses from far impoverished tropical villages and from a stricken Ireland of the past.

And the agony increased as he writhed and rolled with his face contorted into a mask of pain. He tried to gasp out a cry for help but all coherence choked in his throat as the agony gripped every inch of his being. It surged through him but, in particular, it gnawed unceasingly into his stomach. Open-mouthed, gasping, he rolled on the harsh grass . . .

* * *

Young Garda Larry Donovan drove the police car through a bright spring morning. Beside him, Sergeant Ned Byrne leaned easily with an elbow on the edge of the open passenger window, luxuriating in the warm promise of the day.

The car was cruising along the road out of Ballygrill and approaching the point where the old D'Albert lands met the road. Following an annual duty laid on the officers of *Garda Siochana* in rural postings, the two were touring the district to remind holders of the scattered houses that it was the time when certain thistles sprouted and they must clear their gardens or neighboring roadside verges of the weeds whose blown seeds were a menace to the cultivated fields of their farming neighbors. Normally, one officer could undertake the task but, on this pleasant morning, the middle-aged sergeant could not resist an opportunity of abandoning the paperwork on his desk for a spell.

He was enjoying a pleasant reverie when he was abruptly fully awakened to his surroundings by the sight of a figure running along the otherwise empty road, approaching the car with wildly waving arms.

'Who's this and what ails him?' he asked, straining forward in his seat.

'It's old Tommy Lynch, looking as if the devil is after him,' said the younger officer.

Close to the low fieldstone wall, the car halted and Tommy Lynch stumbled to the open window on the sergeant's side, gasping and waving towards the field so carefully shunned by himself and his fellow villagers.

'Come over to the field!' he mouthed. 'Come quick and see what's in it!'

The policemen left the vehicle and hastened with him to look over the wall. Tommy Lynch jabbed a finger towards something lying on one of the overgrown humps that straggled over a portion of the field. 'Look at that! It's a body for sure! I was walking past here when I spotted it. A body in a pair of pyjamas by the look of it.'

'Did you get a close look at it?' asked the sergeant.

'I did not!' stated Lynch with strong emphasis. 'Not for all the tea in China would I set foot in that field!'

'Stay here!' ordered the sergeant. 'We'll talk to you later. 'C'mon, Larry, let's see what we have here.'

The officers climbed the wall and Sergeant Byrne said: 'Listen, lad, whatever you do, don't walk on any of those lumps in the ground. D'you hear me, now? Keep well off them!'

They approached the crumpled object of their attention, sprawled full across one of the grassed mounds. Sure enough, it appeared to be a man clad in pyjamas. They stood over it, bewilderedly, then the sergeant breathed a shocked: 'My God! This can only be the *fir gorta*!'

Larry Donovan felt a quiver of fear course through him, for the man inside the pyjamas could hardly be called a man at all, merely the shriveled husk of one, a bundle of skeletal bones.

'Do you know what this corner of this field is?' asked Sergeant Byrne in an awed tone. 'Do you realize what these humps in the ground are?'

'I don't,' said the younger man. 'I only know there's some kind of superstition about the field and old Mary Crowe says she was attacked by something in it long ago.'

'Graves,' intoned the sergeant weightily. 'Graves are what these bumps are. This bit of the field is a Famine graveyard. About the only humane act of old Lord Hugh D'Albert in the Great Famine was to allow it to be used for the burial of his starved tenants. There's an old, old story clinging to such places. If you walk on a Famine grave, you'll become a victim of the *fir gorta*. Some say it's a stark warning that the Great Famine must never be forgotten and those of a religious complexion will say it's a reminder of the gospels' instruction to feed the hungry.'

Larry Donovan was bending, looking more closely at the grotesque corpse, almost lost in the folds of the night clothing. The head was little more than a skull, but he recognized its anguished, twisted features as those of The Yank, the once hearty, well-fed visitor to the village.

'It's Mr. Criswell, who's taken to

calling himself Criswell D'Albert,' he breathed. 'What in the name of God brought him to this?'

'Name might be the operative word — the name he brought back into these parts,' pronounced his superior. 'Speaking from a non-police point of view, I'd say we're looking at the workings of the old local curse. He somehow got lost among the graves and somehow stumbled over them. So he was caught by the *fir gorta*, poor fellow.' He turned to Donovan, looked at him quizzically and asked: 'I suppose, Dublin jackeen and smart city man though you are, you know what *fir gorta* means?'

'I do, of course, Sergeant, would I be on the force if my Irish wasn't as good as anybody's?' responded Donovan.

And, together, they pronounced the translation: '*Fir gorta* — The Starving Man.'

6

Embrace of Evil

I half expected my twin brother Roger to meet me at Bicester rail station with his car but, when I arrived, there was no sign of him. I shrugged it off as an indication that he was running true to form. Probably, he was so absorbed in his painting or in his ongoing study of art history that he had totally forgotten the time of my train's arrival from London.

My pocket map showed me that the village of Cotstones was only a short distance away and my bag was not heavy so I decided against a taxi thinking that, after my long sojourn in western Canada, it would be good to walk through Oxfordshire lanes on a bright spring day.

A roadside signpost put me on the right path and I was soon strolling between high hedgerows on lanes almost wholly untroubled by traffic. As I progressed, I began to share Roger's enthusiasm for this quiet corner of England where he had rented the old manor house for a time. In several letters written just after his arrival, he praised this rich, green countryside but I was slightly puzzled as to why his letters dropped off after a time. It was typical of a man who lived only for his work that Roger had holed up off the beaten track in an old house without a telephone. It was typical of him, too, that he had no truck with innovations such as e-mail, which he saw as just another nuisance to eat into his precious time. In the last few weeks, our correspondence was limited to a mere couple of letters in which we discussed my plan to visit him when I arrived in England. Strangely, although Roger normally wrote chatty letters, his last ones were unusually terse, as if written by a man who was considerably preoccupied. They carried an almost tangible suggestion of a change in my twin's character and I hoped that he was not overdoing things and was unwell.

Again, among the scented hedgerows

and spring birdsong, this was something I could shrug off. Probably, Roger was just deeply involved in both his painting career, now paying dividends after his early struggles, and his studies of English Victorian art, a field in which he had already produced a couple of well received books. Indeed, I often felt that, when not engrossed before his own easel, my brother lived in the Nineteenth Century world of Rossetti, Burne-Jones, Whistler and Sickert. On the whole, it was a mode of life to which he was totally suited, being a bachelor with a happy-go-lucky attitude, caring little for material possessions.

I mounted a slight rise in the road and spotted a cluster of houses some distance beyond it, obviously the village of Cotstones. At that moment, too, I made my first human contact since leaving Bicester: an elderly man in rough working clothes, walking towards me.

'Am I on the right road for Cotstones Manor?' I called.

He came a little closer and eyed me narrowly from under bushy brows before answering almost suspiciously: 'The

Manor House? Aye, just a bit the other side of the village. You can see the roof from a little way down the road. I'll come back with you and show you.'

He walked beside me toward the village; a friendly gesture, I thought, but I soon found it was mingled with a countryman's curiosity concerning strangers. 'You might well be a brother to the artist chap living at the Manor,' he commented candidly. 'You look just like him — except for the beard and him being thinner than you.'

Beard? Then I recalled that in one of his chattier letters, Roger had said that, since he was now conquering London's Cork Street galleries, he might as well conform to the popular notion of a painter and grow a beard. Thinner? Roger and I normally shared a fairly solid build as well as healthy appetites. If he was now thinner, I hoped it was not because he was neglecting himself.

I satisfied the man's curiosity. 'Yes, I am his brother — his twin, in fact.'

'Ah, I thought as much. You a painter, too?'

'No, nothing so glamorous. I lecture at a university in Canada and I'm home for a few weeks for the first time in three years. What's this about my brother looking thin? Have you heard that he's been ill?'

'No, I don't see a lot of him, but then none of us does. Keeps himself to himself but the wife's sister has the little shop here in the village and he goes there for his various needs. She's mentioned a time or two that he seems to be looking more peaked. And — and, well — he was as friendly a man as you could meet when he first came here but now he's much more stand-offish and silent, as if he doesn't want to have much to do with anyone. I hope you don't mind my mentioning it. Don't think I'm passing judgment on him.'

'No, not at all. It doesn't sound like the brother I know so well. Maybe he isn't so well after all.'

'I wouldn't know but I shouldn't be surprised but what some ailment might come upon a man living in that place.'

'Why — is there something wrong with

Cotstones Manor?'

The old man gave a low and mysterious chuckle. 'Well, let's just say there's stories about it.'

'Stories?'

'Aye, the kind of stories you get in the country. My grandfather told me a lot when I was a boy. He lived to be over ninety and he had dozens of the old yarns from hereabouts, most of which are now long forgotten. But the one about the Manor still lingers.'

'What's the story?' I asked but he pointedly ignored me and stopped me in mid stride, pointing to a pair of high chimneys visible through a gap in the trees beyond the last houses of the village street.

'That's the Manor,' he said. 'I must leave you now. I hope you find your brother well.'

There was something profoundly disturbing in the way he turned hastily and retraced his steps along the street even as I was in the act of thanking him for his help.

I walked onward half-heartedly noting

the surroundings: a small shop; a timbered pub with the sign: *The Plough*; a straggle of cottages, some with new looking extensions and equally new concrete driveways bearing substantial cars, indicating how the rural folk were being replaced by the prosperous crew from the cities and a square-towered Norman church with a sign giving the latest standing of the roof preservation fund. All the time, I thought of Roger and the unpleasant reputation the Cotstones Manor hinted at by my acquaintance from the village.

I found the Manor to be an early Georgian structure, almost lost amid ill-kept trees and shielded from the lane by a high, forbidding wall in a poor state of repair. It was reached by a long pathway, robbed of sunlight by an archway of tall trees. My field is anthropology and at least once before I had encountered the feel of real evil. It was during a field-trip to Mexico, on the site of a place of Aztec sacrifice where the hearts had been torn out of living human victims. The mingled cruelty, violence, terror and pain from centuries before hung in the air like an almost tangible fog. Walking along that path to the forbidding, crumbling old house, I knew something of the same breathtaking revulsion I experienced on that occasion.

Why on earth had Roger rented this ghastly place?

I climbed a set of broad, cracked steps to a great oaken door, which swung open even as I approached. Roger was framed in the portal, a Roger greatly changed since our last meeting. He was certainly much thinner with an unkempt beard and there was an unusual light in his eyes. He was dressed untidily in a stained check shirt, paint-stained trousers and scuffed sandals.

'Oh, it's you, Vic,' he said in a colorless voice as if I were someone who called a couple of times a day rather than the brother whom he had not seen for three years.

'Hello, Roger. Did you get my letter?'

'Yes, come in. Sorry I couldn't meet you at Bicester. Got some trouble with the car.' There was that same flatness to his voice, which seemed to indicate that he couldn't care less whether I turned up or not. 'Come in. I'll organize some tea.'

We passed into a wide hallway holding an almost overpowering mustiness A broad stairway swept down to its center but, where it must once have boasted elegant banister rails, it now had more modern ones of wood, incongruous and rickety-looking. The whole place was grimy and uninviting with oddments of old furniture scattered about. Whoever rented out this unprepossessing place had a nerve making it available and Roger must have been out of his mind to take it.

'Come upstairs,' said Roger. 'My studio's up there and I sleep there too — but I've fixed up a camp bed for you in the next room.'

This room proved to be as untidy and cluttered as the rest of the house with a number of canvases propped against the wall and facing inward. I threw my bag on the camp bed and, while Roger went off to fill the kettle, I turned one of the canvases towards me.

I beheld a painting of the head and

shoulders of a girl, obviously by my brother but a vast improvement over all his earlier work. The subject was a stunning beauty, dressed in the fashion of about 1850. Roger had caught a gently molded, full-lipped face with huge eyes, holding a deep sadness and yet, incongruously, a distinct hardness. I considered the portrait for fully five minutes, realizing that my brother must surely have reached the zenith of his talent.

From another canvas, the same girl looked out at me with the same superbly rendered melancholy. And she was depicted in another, another and yet another. Every canvas showed the same beautiful girl, whose wide eyes held that same melancholy mingled with the jarring quality I began to find menacing.

It looked as if Roger had recently painted nothing but this intriguing and tragic girl over and over again. Whoever she is, I thought, he is obviously *haunted* by her.

Engrossed in the portraits, I almost forgot Roger until I saw him in the doorway, holding a tray bearing cups of tea. A frown crossed his face for a moment as if he was annoyed by my taking the liberty of looking at his work, but he asked: 'Like them?'

'They're terrific,' I told him. 'They're far better than anything you've ever done. Is the model a local girl?'

Roger gave a wry smile. 'Yes, you could say that, Vic — a local girl.'

He sank into silence, obviously not inclined to tell me anything further about the girl who had modeled for the paintings, which must have occupied a great part of his recent time. His stolid silence as we drank tea, together with his gaunt physical appearance and his general air of neglect was now worrying me deeply. This was not the vigorous and carefree Roger with whom I had grown up. Moreover, this welcome, which was hardly any welcome at all, was not what I had expected. In the old days, Roger would almost immediately have whisked me off to the village pub for a meal and drinks and eager conversation. Now, I had the distinct impression that he was only just tolerating me.

Into the bargain, I was concerned about the condition of this half-empty, creepy mansion. Stark bohemian existence might be acceptable among struggling artists but my brother was well established and by no means poor. There was no need for him to live like this.

I tried to broach the subject carefully: 'Roger, why are you living in this place? From what I see of it, you haven't even any electricity here. I've noticed only oil lamps.'

'Because I was attracted to it,' he answered sharply. 'There is something here that attracted me from the first time I set eyes on the house.'

The words made me shudder. I somehow felt that it was this house that was turning my brother into almost a shadow of his old self. It was essential that I got him away from the place but I knew Roger's stubborn streak. He was always a hard man to persuade against his wishes and it was evident that whatever attracted him to Cotstones Manor was likely to hold him hard.

He slammed down his teacup as if

closing our conversation. 'I'll go downstairs and fix something to eat,' he announced. 'I have the kitchen down there fitted out to my satisfaction. And the bathroom is just along the corridor if you want to clean up. It's not luxurious but, again, it's to my satisfaction.'

I was left alone, watching the first shades of evening descending behind the high window and wondering how I could persuade him to leave oppressive Cotstones Manor, a place wherein I myself had no desire to spend any more time than I need.

Bewilderedly, I eventually went along the musty and shadowy corridor to find the bathroom. It proved just about adequate with fittings at least eighty years old and I washed hastily.

Then, as I returned along the corridor, I saw her.

The girl in Roger's paintings was standing in the gloom close to the door of his studio. She was in a crinoline of sumptuous material, with her hair braided and with ribbons in the style of the 1850s and her face was every bit as beautiful as my brother had rendered it on canvas — until she fixed me with her large eyes, whereupon her expression changed to one of utter hatred. Her whole countenance was a malevolent mask, telling me I was not wanted here.

I was frozen on the spot, trying to understand how she came to be there and yet knowing that, while she looked solid, she was not really there at all — at least not in a fully physical sense. Abruptly, she turned her back on me in eloquent disdain and walked away but it was not so much a walk as a slow, halting stumble. Under her crinoline finery, this girl from another century must have been dreadfully maimed.

Then, right before my eyes, she faded and was gone.

Shaking, I returned to the room Roger had given me and found him there with sandwiches and fresh tea. One of the oil lamps was now lit and its glow emphasized his gaunt and unkempt appearance. I leaned against the doorjamb, trying to regain my composure.

'I've just had a strange experience,' I

told him, hearing a cracked note in my own voice. 'I've seen the girl in your paintings — out there in the corridor!'

'You've seen Rosalind? You can't have! Only I have seen her!' Roger's response was almost a snarl.

I gripped the doorjamb firmly. I was still shivering and a well remembered sensation was creeping over me — that same perception of evil that I felt when I first walked the path to Cotstones Manor, more intense now. It bid fair to overpower me, an almost physical, thrusting force, aimed at me and calculated to drive me away. I knew it emanated from the apparition I encountered in the corridor.

'I *have* seen her, Roger,' I heard myself gasping. 'I never thought I'd ever say it but I've seen a ghost. The girl in your portraits is a ghost and the vile atmosphere of this rotten place issues from her. For God's sake get out of here, man!'

Roger was crouching forward, menacing in the uncertain lamplight. 'Yes, she's a ghost,' he breathed. 'She's an unfortunate shade who hung around this place for decade after decade as the place all but crumbled away; a forgotten wraith from another time who had nothing but pain, disappointment, misunderstanding and bitterness in her own day. I know it was she who drew me here. I felt her presence the first time I laid eyes on the place and finding her was the greatest thing ever to happen to me. Ghost she might be, but she inspired me to create my best work ever. I'm content here with Rosalind and if anyone should get out it's you. We don't want you here, Rosalind and I. Go on — clear out!'

The oppressive force of evil was wrapping me like a blanket. I needed air. I needed to get out of this place and be among sane mortals but I saw something in a diamond bright light.

'My God — you're in love with a ghost!' I gasped. 'She's taken you over. You're besotted by her. No wonder you're reclusive and are becoming nothing but skin and bone. You're in the grip of something not of this world.'

'Clear out!' my brother shouted. 'Go on! Get out!'

I tried to shake off the weight of the sense of malevolence like a drowning man attempting to find air, turned and somehow forced myself to stagger out to the stairs. As I went, I had a last glimpse of Roger. But he was not alone.

The ghost-girl was standing behind him, bestowing on me a triumphant parting smile, laden with ill will. She seemed to be fondling his shoulders with hands that I knew were not of flesh and blood.

And I was sure I heard a soft feminine voice murmur:

'*Soon, Roger! Soon we will be together and free of this wretched world.*'

I staggered out of the Manor and along the gloomy path with its forbidding arch of trees to burst into the deserted lane, shrouded by early evening. Once out of the place, the crushing depression lifted. I leaned against the long garden wall and tried to collect my thoughts. I must get Roger out of Cotstones Manor somehow. I must break the grip of the ghost girl, rid him of his infatuation with her and return him to where he belonged in the healthy world of sunlight and flesh and blood affairs.

But how? I needed time to think and to be away from the vicinity of Cotstones Manor. I also needed a steadying drink and the company of ordinary, no-nonsense people. I thought of the local pub, *The Plough*, and made for it.

I entered a busy bar, with a good number of customers who had the look of incomers, the well-heeled city types who had settled in the village. I slumped against the bar and asked for a neat whisky. Then I spotted the local who had welcomed me to the village, sitting with a crony, well apart from the brash incomers.

The countrymen were eying me with deep interest and I supposed my disturbed state was all too obvious. I downed the whisky quickly, feeling some satisfaction from its warmth and I crossed to the pair and sat beside him.

'Listen,' I said to the old man of my earlier acquaintance, 'that business of the Manor house — what's the whole story?'

'Why?' he asked breathlessly. 'Has

something happened up there?'

'The story!' I demanded impatiently. 'Has it something to do with a young woman?'

'Aye, it has,' put in his companion eagerly. 'All the old folk years ago knew the yarn. It concerned the daughter of the house, belonging to the Courcey family who once owned the land hereabouts.'

'A beautiful girl, badly crippled in an accident,' said the friend I had made earlier. 'Terrible tragic, the old people always said, though others claimed what happened to her was a dreadful form of justice like that in the Bible. For beautiful she might be but she was a willful girl, a schemer who stole another young woman's sweetheart and broke her heart. Just as bad as coveting another's wife — that's how them who'd pass judgment on her saw it.'

Between them, they gave me the story, a stark one, laden with severe peasant morality. Rosalind Courcey who was pampered and believed she could take whatever she fancied, set her cap at a young officer from an equally autocratic family. He was all but betrothed to another girl but Rosalind's beauty enticed him away. She flaunted her conquest before all the fashionable society but, only weeks before their marriage, tragedy struck. Returning to the manor house from a ball one stormy winter night, she was stepping down from her coach when the thunder and lightning frightened the horses. They bolted along the drive but the girl's shawl had somehow become entangled in a handle on the coach door and she was dragged under the wheels.

She was almost killed but she survived with dreadfully mangled legs. Her days of walking haughtily through country and London society were gone — and so was her gallant young officer, who eventually became a general well known to history. His love, such as it was, did not extend to taking on the responsibility of an invalid wife.

Rosalind became a recluse in Cotstones Manor, growing increasingly embittered until, one day, she took her own life.

'And you know how country folk thought long ago,' said my first acquaintance. 'They believed there was no rest for suicides — though I never considered that a charitable notion. However, long after all the Courceys passed away and the old Manor fell more into ruin, there was a belief that Rosalind haunted the place. And it was no more than she deserved, said the Bible-thumpers, for she was a scheming Jezebel at heart and she'd died by her own hand.'

'That's a harsh judgment on the poor girl,' growled his companion, taking a pull of his beer. 'She deserved some sympathy. Not that her ghost was ever actually seen. Them who dared to enter the house reckoned her presence was felt more than seen. She might be seen, though, if all the conditions were right — or wrong, so to speak.'

I had heard enough. My thoughts were whirling and without a word of farewell, I left the two men and rushed into the street. One clear resolution swam to the top of my tangled consciousness: I must get Roger out of that house, even if I had to knock him flat and drag him out. I strode determinedly along the village street.

'*If the conditions were right*,' the countryman had said. Perhaps Roger brought such conditions to Cotstones Manor. His artistic studies meant that, mentally, he lived almost constantly in the Nineteenth Century, so maybe he was so sensitively attuned to the period that he tapped into whatever supernatural circuit made Rosalind Courcey manifest where others never saw her. Possibly, through the natural affinity of twins, I had the same sensitivity and so I, too, was aware of her.

At all events, she was certainly *there* for both of us and a malignant menace to the pair of us — particularly to Roger, whom she had plainly ensnared. From all the signs, he was in love with this wraith from an era long gone. Consumed by a raging desire to free my brother from the ghost-girl, I charged along the now almost black, tree-arched pathway, feeling the aura of evil intensify as I neared the dark bulk of the house.

Trying to shut out its oppressive pressure, I blundered through the still open front door and stumbled up the stairs to where a chink of lamplight showed at the door of the studio. I crashed in, yelling: 'Roger! Listen to me — you must leave this damned place! I don't know what the motives of your ghost-woman are, but local folklore has her down as an embittered, scheming spirit and she certainly makes this place hideous. Get loose from her, man . . . '

'I thought I'd seen the last of you, Vic,' cut in Roger at the top of his voice. He was still standing in the middle of the room, looking yet more eerie in the lamp-glow and Rosalind was hovering behind him, appearing even more solid, fixing me with her glare of hatred and yet with a mocking half-smile. 'What the hell do you know about it?' my brother harangued. 'I was content here with Rosalind until you turned up. Yes, she's a ghost, a specter or whatever you want to call her but, if you can believe it, I am able to show her some of the affection she was robbed of long ago. And she is good for me. She has inspired me to do my finest work. I have put the beauty of this broken, scorned and maligned girl on canvas after canvas for all posterity and . . . '

'*And, soon, we will be together for all time, your brother and I,*' concluded the hollow, mocking voice of the ghost-girl. '*I shall see to that, depend on it.*'

Now, through my tortured fear and anger, I realized something new. Roger was besotted with Rosalind Courcey and physically reduced almost to a shadow by his infatuation. This malignant, man-stealing Jezebel of local peasant legend plainly intended to have a farther effect and take his very life — to enable him to join her on whatever eternal plane she inhabited.

I wanted to knock Roger senseless and haul him away from her presence, from this room and out of this ghastly house. Hardly knowing what I was doing, I lunged at him with my fists, trying to hit his bearded chin. But he was ready for me and he thumped me heftily in the chest, sending me staggering backwards towards the open door. From the small table near his easel, he snatched up a pallet-knife with its thin, sharp blade and charged forward.

As he swung it in a wide arc, I jumped back yet further and now I was on the landing, falling against the rickety wooden banister rail, substituting for the elegant antique rails that must once have graced the stairway. And Roger followed up his attack, barging into me while I grabbed his arm and tried to force him to drop the knife.

Then, with a tortured groan and a crack, the rotten wood gave way and we were pitching back into empty space. We hit the floor of the shadow-invaded hall below and I knew I had fallen on top of my brother. Winded, but seemingly unhurt, I staggered up. I realized that Roger was gasping and trying to get to his feet.

I tried to help him then realized that Rosalind Courcey was crouching beside him, fondling his head possessively and looking up at me with her lip curling contemptuously.

'Go away!' I yelled. 'Go away! Leave him alone!'

Consumed by my desire to drive the ghost away, I snatched up a broken stave of banister rail and lashed out at her hands, delivering blow upon blow, oblivious to the fact that physical force has no effect on specters — or that I was striking through her, onto my brother's head!

The policemen, a seasoned sergeant and a hefty young constable, emerged from somewhere beyond my curtain of enraged tears and it later transpired that they were traveling the lane in their patrol car when they heard me yelling inside the house. The constable wrested the length of wood from my hand and yanked me to my feet. He forced my hands behind my back, growling: 'Damn it, man, what're you trying to do, beat him to death?'

The sergeant, kneeling beside Roger's still form, grunted: 'Looks like he's already done that, lad. This chap's stone dead.'

From the gloom, the shade of Rosalind Courcey, visible only to myself, taunted me with her smirk of triumph.

'You don't expect a learned judge and a jury of sober citizens to swallow yarns about ghosts, do you?' sneered the Crown Court prosecutor into my face. 'Isn't it the simple truth that you had a furious row with your brother and launched a murderous attack on him? The officers caught you in the act and they saw nothing of this ghost you claim you were trying to drive away.'

Unlikely though my tale was, it was given some support by Ted Ferris and Jack Kenwood, the villagers from the pub. They volunteered themselves as defense witnesses, saying there was indeed a local legend of the ghost of Cotstones Manor. Old locals, whom the smart-alecky incomers called 'yokels,' knew it and gave the house a wide berth. Their intervention had some effect on the judge who asked me several times whether I really believed I saw the ghost-girl.

Instructing the jury, he made play of my possible mental state. 'You might feel that this story of the defendant trying to drive away a malignant spirit is nonsense but it is not impossible that he was suffering from some temporary mental aberration, though he has no history of such disturbance,' he pronounced. 'If you feel that to be so, you would be wrong to conclude that Victor Hayles *willfully* murdered his brother, Roger Hayles, and therefore the statutory prison sentence would be inappropriate . . . '

So, I was shown some leniency, sent to where I write this, a secure hospital rather than a prison. My sentence is indefinite and, every day of it, I am haunted by the last sight to impress itself upon me as the police took me out of that hideous house.

In the gloom of the hall, the shades of Rosalind Courcey, dead for more than a century and a half, and my newly dead brother were embracing.

And I know that Cotstones Manor now has *two* ghosts

THE END

We do hope that you have enjoyed reading this large print book.

Did you know that all of our titles are available for purchase?

We publish a wide range of high quality large print books including:
Romances, Mysteries, Classics
General Fiction
Non Fiction and Westerns

Special interest titles available in large print are:
The Little Oxford Dictionary
Music Book, Song Book
Hymn Book, Service Book

Also available from us courtesy of Oxford University Press:
Young Readers' Dictionary
(large print edition)
Young Readers' Thesaurus
(large print edition)

For further information or a free brochure, please contact us at:
Ulverscroft Large Print Books Ltd.,
The Green, Bradgate Road, Anstey,
Leicester, LE7 7FU, England.
Tel: (00 44) **0116 236 4325**
Fax: (00 44) **0116 234 0205**

Other titles in the
Linford Mystery Library:

THE TWISTED TONGUES

John Burke

A wartime traitor who broadcast from Germany is finally released from prison. Nobody wanted to listen to him during the war and nobody wants to listen to him now. But he intends to be heard, and when he begins to write his memoirs for a newspaper, old ghosts stir uneasily and it becomes a race against time: will he reveal the truth behind the smug respectability of men in high places before they find a means of silencing him forever?

ANGEL DOLL

Arlette Lees

It's the dark days of the Great Depression, and former Boston P.D. detective Jack Dunning is starting over after losing both his wife and his job to the bottle. Fresh off the Greyhound, he slips into The Blue Rose Dance Hall — and falls hard for a beautiful dime-a-dance girl, Angel Doll. But then Angel shoots gangster Axel Teague and blows town on the midnight train to Los Angeles . . .

THE INFERNAL DEVICE

Michael Kurland

Professor Moriarty, erstwhile Mathematics professor, is not 'the greatest rogue unhanged' that Sherlock Holmes would have one believe, but rather an amoral genius — and the only man Holmes has ever been bested by. *The Infernal Device* takes Professor Moriarty from London to Stamboul to Moscow and back, Sherlock Holmes close on his tail, until they both join forces to pursue and capture a man more devious and more dangerous than either of them has ever faced before . . .

I AM ISABELLA

V. J. Banis

It seems an innocent enough deception — pretend to be the absent heiress, Isabella Hale, just for one evening. And certainly the objective is a noble one — to present a generous check to an unquestionably deserving charity. As it turns out, however, Carol Andrews' identity is not the only thing that isn't all it seems. In no time at all, she finds herself in a high-stakes game of deceit and danger, in which she faces the ultimate penalty — death . . .